R.L - 5.0
PLs - 5.0
Quiz # - 115
840L

P9-CET-871

The Great Brain
Does It Again

Books by John D. Fitzgerald

THE GREAT BRAIN DOES IT AGAIN

THE RETURN OF THE GREAT BRAIN

THE GREAT BRAIN REFORMS

THE GREAT BRAIN AT THE ACADEMY

ME AND MY LITTLE BRAIN

MORE ADVENTURES OF THE GREAT BRAIN

THE GREAT BRAIN

BRAVE BUFFALO FIGHTER

PRIVATE EYE

UNCLE WILL AND THE FITZGERALD CURSE

PAPA MARRIED A MORMON

MAMMA'S BOARDING HOUSE

THE DIAL PRESS  NEW YORK

The Great Brain Does It Again

Brentwood Union School Dist.

ILLUSTRATED BY MERCER MAYER

Garin School

by John D. Fitzgerald

3581

Text copyright © 1975 by John D. Fitzgerald
Illustrations copyright © 1975 by The Dial Press
All rights reserved. No part of this book may be
reproduced in any form or by any means without the
prior written permission of the publisher, excepting brief
quotes used in connection with reviews written
specifically for inclusion in a magazine or newspaper.
Printed in the United States of America · Second Printing 1976

Library of Congress Cataloging in Publication Data
Fitzgerald, John Dennis. The great brain does it again.
Summary: In turn-of-the-century Mormon Utah, Tom's
great brain comes up with eight more schemes, most of
them concerned with earning money. [1. Humorous stories]
I. Mayer, Mercer, 1943–   ill.   II. Title.
PZ7.F57535Gu [Fic]   74–18600
ISBN 0-8037-5065-X   ISBN 0-8037-5066-8 lib. bdg.

T 68153

For Ann Elmo

Contents

The Great Brain
Does It Again

CHAPTER ONE

The Buried Treasure Swindle

MY BROTHER TOM knew the A, B, C's, could write numbers from one to one hundred, spell a lot of words, and read simple sentences before he started school. He did get some help from Papa and Mamma and my oldest brother Sweyn, but he learned most of these things by himself.

Mrs. Thatcher taught the first through the sixth grades in our one-room schoolhouse when Tom started school. Adenville, Utah, had a population of about two thousand Mormons, four hundred Protestants, and only about a hundred of us Catholics, so a one-room schoolhouse was all we needed. Later, after Mrs. Thatcher retired, Mr. Standish became our teacher. He let Tom skip the fifth grade. I guess that proves how smart my brother was.

Before 1898 any parents wanting their children to get more than a sixth-grade education had to send them away from home to go to school. Papa sent Sweyn and Tom to the Jesuit Catholic Academy for Boys in Salt Lake City, where the seventh and eighth grades were taught. After Sweyn graduated from the eighth grade, Papa sent him to Boylestown, Pennsylvania, to live with relatives and go to high school. Tom didn't have to return to the academy for eighth grade. A nondenominational academy for seventh and eighth graders had been built in Adenville that year. Thirty-three students were enrolled. Tom was only twelve years old at the time.

But the trouble with Tom's great brain was his money-loving heart. Everybody laughed when, at the age of eight, he started telling people he had a great brain. But after he began to use his great brain to swindle kids and make fools out of adults, nobody laughed at him anymore. Us kids put up with him until he was twelve. Then he went too far. For thirty cents he put the lives of my two best friends in danger. We put him on trial in our barn and he was found guilty of being a confidence man, a crook, a swindler, and a blackmailer. The sentence handed down was that no kid in town would play with him or have anything to do with him for one year unless he gave up his crooked ways. The fellows let Tom off the hook when he promised to reform.

But did he reform? Heck no. Oh, he had Papa and Mamma and the kids fooled, but not me. It was just that the swindles he pulled off were so slick that nobody could prove they were swindles.

The Adenville Academy was two blocks from the Common School, where my adopted brother Frankie and I went to

4

school. Frankie was in the first grade. I was in the fifth grade. Frankie's parents and brother had been killed in a rockslide when he was four years old. Papa and Mamma had adopted him after my uncle, Mark Trainor, who was the town marshal and a deputy sheriff, couldn't locate any relatives. Frankie was now six. It was easy to see he wasn't my real brother because he had the blackest and straightest hair of any kid in town. I took after Papa and had dark curly hair. Sweyn was a blond like our Danish mother. Tom was a sort of mixture of Papa and Mamma and the only one who had freckles.

It was the first Friday in November when this buried treasure scheme of Tom's began. He met us on the corner after school. We stopped at the *Adenville Weekly Advocate* office to find out if Papa wanted Tom to help him. Papa was editor and publisher of the town's only newspaper and did printing for everybody who needed it. He was setting type when we entered the office.

"Want me to come back and help after I change clothes?" Tom asked.

Papa looked at us from beneath his green eyeshade. "No, thanks, T. D.," he said. "But I'll need your help next week on a big printing job."

My brothers and I usually called each other by our first and middle initials because that's how Papa usually addressed us. We all had the same middle name of Dennis just like Papa because it was a family tradition.

Mamma and Aunt Bertha were in the kitchen making pies when we got home. Mamma had her blond hair piled high in braids on her head like she usually wore it. Aunt Bertha wasn't really our aunt. She came to live with us after her husband died because she didn't have any place to go and she wasn't a Mormon. The Church of Jesus Christ of Latter-day Saints took care of any Mormon in need, but Aunt Bertha was a Methodist. Why she picked our family, which was Catholic, I'll never know. She simply walked into Papa's newspaper office one day after burying her husband and said she had no place to go. She was a big woman in her sixties with hands and feet as big as a man's. In a short time she became like one of the family.

Aunt Bertha being a Methodist and us being Catholics never bothered us. The Mormons had their tabernacle church with Bishop Aden because Adenville was what they called a ward. But us Catholics and Protestants didn't have any church of our own. We all went to the Community Church, where Reverend Holcomb preached strictly from the Bible so he wouldn't show favoritism to any religion. Once a year the Protestants had a revival meeting at the campground when a traveling evangelist came to town. And once a year a Jesuit missionary priest came to Adenville, where he listened to confessions, held masses, baptized babies, and married Catholics in the Community Church.

Mamma got the cookie jar from the pantry and put it on the kitchen table while Aunt Bertha got a pitcher of milk from the icebox.

"Have your cookies and milk," Mamma said, "and then I have something to tell you."

No wonder Mamma gave us the cookies and milk first. For Tom and me it was the same as giving a condemned man a hearty meal before hanging him.

"I want the vegetable garden turned over tomorrow," Mamma said after we'd finished.

6

We should have expected this because it happened every fall after the growing season ended. Due to the mild climate in Adenville we could grow vegetables until about the middle of October. Last Saturday Tom and I had worked all day hauling manure from our barn and corral to spread on the garden. Tomorrow we would have to spade the garden a shovelful at a time, burying the manure beneath the dirt. This would fertilize the garden for planting in the spring.

"Can't it wait until next weekend?" Tom asked. "J. D. and I worked all last Saturday hauling and spreading manure."

"No, it can't," Mamma said. "I'm getting too many flies from the manure."

We knew there was no appeal to one of Mamma's decisions. A criminal could appeal to a higher court, but could a kid? Heck no. For my money there just wasn't any justice in this world for kids. Mamma had put up with the flies for a week. It wouldn't have hurt her to put up with them for another week instead of making Tom and me work like slaves two Saturdays in a row.

I followed Tom and Frankie upstairs to our bedroom where we changed to our playclothes. Then we went and sat on the back porch steps. We had a very large backyard divided by a wooden sidewalk that led from our back porch to our coal-and-woodshed. The left side we used as a playground. The right side was the vegetable garden, and the longer I looked at it the bigger it seemed. Beyond the coal-and-woodshed were our chicken coop, toolshed, barn, and corral.

Eddie Huddle came over to play with Frankie. Tom and I just sat staring at the vegetable garden. I couldn't help thinking it was tough enough for a fellow to have to go to school five days a week without having to work two Saturdays in a row. And I knew from the expression on Tom's face that he was putting his great brain to work on how to bamboozle me into spading the garden by myself.

"Tell you what I'm going to do, J. D.," he said as he put his arm around my shoulders. "Out of the goodness of my heart I'm going to let you spade the garden by yourself and keep the half-dollar Papa always gives us for doing it."

Fifty cents was a fortune in those days. But I knew it would take me all day Saturday and part of Sunday to spade the garden by myself. And besides, every time Tom started talking about the goodness of his heart, I always ended up with the worst of the deal.

"You aren't going to bamboozle me into spading the garden by myself," I said.

"Who's trying to bamboozle you?" Tom demanded as if I'd accused him of stealing candy from a two year old. "I made you a business proposition and a darn good one."

"If it is so darn good," I said, "I'll tell you what I'm going to do. You spade the garden and you can have my twenty-five cents."

"You've got yourself a deal," Tom said. "Shake on it."

And before I could stop him he grabbed my hand and shook it to seal the bargain. I'd only said what I did because I was sure he would turn the offer down.

"No deal," I said. "I need that quarter to help buy a new air rifle."

Tom shook his head sadly. "When the news gets around town you won't have one friend left," he said. "None of the fellows will speak to you or have anything to do with you."

"What news?" I asked.

8

"That you are a welcher," Tom said. "A fellow who gives his word and shakes hands to seal a bargain and then backs out. I've certainly got to let the fellows know about it."

Boy, oh, boy, what a mess me and my big mouth had gotten me into. I knew that by the time Tom got through telling it no kid in town would have anything to do with me. To the fellows a welcher was about as popular as a wild skunk in a parlor. Tom had me over a barrel.

"All right," I said. "It is a deal. But I'm going to enjoy sitting right on these back porch steps and watching you work like a dog spading the garden."

"Watching me spade the garden?" Tom asked as if I had beans rattling around inside my head instead of brains. "My great brain has been working on a plan to get the garden spaded since last Saturday."

"But the deal was that you would spade the garden," I protested.

"No, it wasn't," Tom said. "You said if I did it that I could have your quarter. You didn't say how I had to do it. As long as the garden gets spaded that is all that counts." He stood up. "Come on, let's go to Smith's vacant lot and play until it's time to do the chores."

Seth Smith's father owned a big vacant lot almost half a block square. He let us kids use it as a playground in return for keeping it cleared of weeds. There were about twenty kids there when we arrived. Tom called to Danny Forester, Parley Benson, Seth Smith, and Pete Kyle, who were playing scrub football with some other kids.

"How would you fellows like to go on a buried treasure hunt tomorrow morning?" he asked.

Danny had something the matter with his left eyelid. It

was always half closed unless he was excited, angry, or surprised. Then it would flip wide open.

"How can you have a buried treasure in Utah, where there have never been any pirates?" he asked.

"You don't need pirates to have a buried treasure," Tom said.

Parley Benson, who wore his coonskin cap all the time when he was outside except when he went in swimming, pushed it to the back of his head.

"What are you getting at, Tom?" he asked.

"You four fellows come to my place tomorrow morning after chores and I'll show you," Tom said. "And make sure you all bring a shovel with you to dig for the buried treasure."

We played until it was time to go home and do the evening chores. Pete Kyle, who lived east of the railroad tracks, walked with us down Main Street. It was a wide street like in most Utah towns, covered with a foot of gravel so it wouldn't be muddy when it rained. There were wooden sidewalks and hitching posts in front of the places of business, and the street was lined with trees planted by early Mormon pioneers. Most of the businesses and homes were west of the railroad tracks, which separated the town. East of the tracks were a couple of saloons, the Palace Cafe, the Sheepmen's Hotel, a rooming house, a livery stable, a few homes, a couple of stores, and the campgrounds. Our home was on Main Street on the west side just a block from the business district. Tom stopped in front of our house to talk to Pete. I went around into the backyard. Eddie Huddle, who had been playing with Frankie, said it was time for him to go home. I sat on the back porch steps with Frankie waiting for Tom so we could do the evening chores.

10

I only had a little brain, but I knew Tom's great brain had come up with a scheme to get those four fellows to spade our vegetable garden. But the buried treasure part didn't make any more sense to me than a bird trying to fly backwards.

"Boy, oh, boy," I said when Tom joined us, "when those fellows find out there is no buried treasure in our vegetable garden, they are going to be plenty mad at you."

"Who says there isn't a buried treasure there?" Tom asked.

"I do," I said. "I've helped to spade the garden ever since I was old enough. There couldn't be a buried treasure there or we would have found it a long time ago."

"Then put your money where your mouth is," Tom said. "Bet you a quarter that Parley, or Seth, or Pete, or Danny find a buried treasure in our vegetable garden."

Every time I'd put my money where my mouth is with Tom I'd lost the bet. But this was one time I knew I'd win. Tom was just trying to stop me from telling the fellows they were being bamboozled into spading the garden for him.

"A buried treasure means money or jewels," I said.

"And I'm betting one of the treasure hunters finds money or jewels worth at least a dollar," Tom said.

"You've got yourself a bet," I said.

The next morning after chores Tom got four stakes from the woodshed. He divided the garden into four equal parts by drawing lines in the manure and dirt. Then he used the stakes to number each quarter of the garden from one to four. He had just finished when Seth, Pete, Danny, and Parley arrived.

Tom pointed at the garden. "You have my word of honor," he said, "that someplace in the vegetable garden there is a tin can with a silver dollar in it. That is the buried treasure. The first one to find it gets to keep the dollar. But there are certain rules for the buried treasure hunt. I want the garden spaded just as if it was your own."

Parley leaned on his shovel handle. "What if one of us finds the buried treasure before the garden is all turned over?" he asked.

"I was coming to that," Tom said. "Before you can join the buried treasure hunt, you must all give me your word of honor that you'll finish spading the garden no matter who finds the buried treasure."

They all gave their word of honor. Then Tom went to the back porch and took a straw from a broom which he broke into four different lengths. He came back holding the four straws so all we could see was the end of each straw.

"I'm the only one who knows where the buried treasure is located," he said. "To make it fair and square you will each draw a straw. The one who gets the longest straw will dig the quarter of the garden marked number one. The next longest the part marked number two, the next number three, and the shortest straw will dig number four. All right, Pete, you go first."

Pete got the longest straw, Danny the next longest, Seth the next, and Parley got the shortest straw.

"All right, fellows," Tom said, "the buried treasure hunt is about to begin. Start in the middle of your quarter and dig towards the ends. Take your places."

The four treasure hunters took their places.

"Let's go, fellows!" Tom shouted. "And see who has the

12

lucky shovel that will find the buried treasure."

Boy, oh, boy, I'll bet Parley, Danny, Seth, and Pete had never worked so hard and so fast digging their own vegetable gardens. They were really making the dirt fly as I sat on the back porch steps with Tom and Frankie watching them.

"Is there really a silver dollar in a tin can buried in the garden?" I asked Tom, because it didn't make sense to me.

"I buried it there this morning while you and Frankie were watering the livestock," Tom answered.

"Then all I can say," I said, "is that your great brain and money-loving heart must have taken a vacation. You'll get fifty cents from Papa and you'll win a quarter from me. That only adds up to seventy-five cents, which means it will cost you a quarter of your own money. You could have gotten Pete to spade the whole garden for fifty cents because his parents are poor."

"I wouldn't make any money on the deal that way," Tom said.

"Well," I said, "I sure as heck don't see how you can make any money this way."

"That is because you've only got a little brain," Tom said.

Just then Mamma came out on the back porch. She stared at the four boys busily spading the garden.

"Just what is going on here?" she demanded.

"You said you wanted the garden turned over this morning," Tom said.

"But why are those four boys doing it instead of you and John D.?" Mamma asked.

Frankie spoke before Tom could answer. "They are looking for a buried treasure," he said.

"Tom Dennis," Mamma said, using his full name which meant she was angry, "is this another of your schemes after you promised to reform? Buried treasure indeed."

"I give you my word, Mamma," Tom said, "that one of the fellows is going to find a tin can with some money in it in the garden. That is the buried treasure. And all of them volunteered as treasure hunters and are perfectly satisfied with the deal."

"I see," Mamma said. "You and John D. knew Papa would give you fifty cents for spading the garden, so you hid fifty cents in it to get out of doing the work. Oh, well, as long as the boys do a good job I guess it will be all right." But she was shaking her head as if she wasn't sure as she went back into the kitchen.

Tom turned on Frankie. "You are getting to be a regular little tattle-tale," he said.

"I wasn't snitching," Frankie said. "I just didn't want Mamma to think you were swindling anybody."

We sat there watching the four treasure hunters working like beavers until about three-fourths of the garden was spaded. Then Pete Kyle turned over a shovelful of dirt and found the tin can. We all crowded around him.

Danny pointed at the can. "We've been swindled," he said. "There is nothing in it but some newspaper."

"That was just to keep the dollar from falling out," Tom said. "Take out the paper, Pete."

And sure enough, on the bottom of the can was a silver dollar. Pete did a happy little jig while the other three treasure hunters watched him with envy.

"Remember the deal, fellows," Tom said. "You've got to finish spading the garden."

14

I walked to our back porch steps with Tom and Frankie as the four fellows went back to work.

"Before you sit down, J. D.," Tom said, "go get that quarter you owe me."

What could I do? I'd lost the bet. I went upstairs and got twenty-five cents from my bank. I returned to the back porch steps and handed the quarter to Tom.

The four fellows finished spading the garden before noon. I couldn't get it out of my head that something was fishy about the whole deal. How could The Great Brain make money on a deal that cost him a dollar when all he got out of it was the fifty cents Papa would give him and the quarter he'd won from me? I became even more suspicious when Danny, Seth, and Parley left but Pete stayed behind. Tom waited until the other three were out of sight.

"Come down to the barn, Pete," he said. "I've got something I want to show you."

I waited until they reached the alley. Then I ran like sixty around our chicken coop to the back of the barn, where there was a big knothole. I put one eye over it and looked inside the barn. I couldn't hear what Pete and Tom were saying but I didn't have to. I saw Pete give the silver dollar to Tom and then Tom gave Pete the quarter he'd won from me.

Boy, oh, boy, what a swindle. Tom would get half a dollar from Papa for spading the garden and the quarter he'd won from me. That gave him a neat profit of fifty cents on the deal and also got him out of spading the garden. I waited until Pete had left for home and then confronted Tom in our backyard.

"I spied on you and Pete," I said. "I saw him give you back the silver dollar and you give him the quarter you won from me. Give me back my quarter or I'll tell Papa and Mamma."

"Let me get this straight," Tom said. "If I don't give you back your quarter you are threatening to tell Mamma and Papa about the whole deal."

"Right," I said.

"In other words," Tom said, "you are trying to blackmail me. Well, go ahead and tell them, J. D., and after you finish I'll tell them how you tried to blackmail me. And for trying to blackmail me, you will get ten times the punishment that I'll get."

He had me and I knew it. But I wasn't about to give up trying to get back my quarter.

"Then I'll tell Parley, Danny, and Seth how you and Pete swindled them," I said. "You fixed the whole thing with Pete yesterday. You let Pete draw the first straw to make sure he got to spade the quarter of the garden where the tin can was buried. You told him yesterday which straw to draw. And I'll tell them about Pete giving you back the dollar and you only giving him a quarter."

"Telling and proving are two different things," Tom said. "Pete isn't going to admit anything for three reasons. First, he gave me his word. Second, he knows that any of the other three fellows can whip him in a fight. And third, Pete is happy with the deal. He only had to spade a quarter of the garden, and twenty-five cents is good pay for that. And if the fellows ask me, I'll tell them that you are just trying to get even with me because I wouldn't let you be one of the treasure hunters. So, you see, J. D., you can't prove a darn thing."

Tom was right. The Great Brain had pulled off another one of his slick swindles and neither his victims nor I could

17

do anything about it. I'd never won a bet from Tom yet, but I'd been stupid enough to bet again. Boy, oh, boy, the fellow who said donkeys were the dumbest of all living creatures had never met a fellow like me.

CHAPTER TWO

The Missing Rocking Horse

JIMMY GRUBER DIED just a few days after Tom had pulled off his buried treasure swindle. His death reminded me of the birthday present Frankie had received when he was five years old. Frankie had let Papa and Mamma know in plenty of time that he wanted a rocking horse for his birthday. He knew it had to be ordered from Sears Roebuck. Papa and Mamma had adopted Frankie when he was four years old, so this was his first birthday as a member of our family. I guess that is why Papa ordered the best rocking horse advertised in the Sears Roebuck catalogue. It was different from any other rocking horse in town. It was what they called a Swing Rocking Horse. The platform stood still and the horse

19

was held by levers so you could swing back and forth on it instead of having rockers like a rocking chair. It was a beauty, with real horsehair for a mane and tail and a leather bridle and saddle. Even kids seven and eight years old wanted to ride it. If Tom had owned it he would have made a fortune charging for rides.

Frankie was also given a cowboy suit by Uncle Mark and Aunt Cathie. When he was dressed in his cowboy suit and riding his rocking horse, Frankie was a real cowboy on a real horse in his imagination. He named the horse Bullet because he said it could run as fast as a bullet fired from a gun. The first week he owned the rocking horse he spent hours riding it and pretending he was a cowboy. He kept it on our front porch and insisted on going out and saying goodnight to Bullet every night before he went to bed.

Then came the Saturday morning when Frankie got dressed in his cowboy suit and went to the front porch to ride Bullet. The rocking horse was missing. He let out a yell that Tom and I heard all the way to our corral. We ran like sixty to the front porch, expecting to find Frankie had fallen off the horse and broken an arm or a leg. Mamma got there before us. She was sitting on the porch swing holding Frankie in her lap. He was crying.

"What's the matter with him?" Tom asked.

"His rocking horse is missing," Mamma answered.

Frankie let out a scream. "I want Bullet!"

Mamma tried to wipe the tears from his eyes with a handkerchief, but he pushed her hand away.

"Now please stop crying, dear," Mamma said. "We will find Bullet."

"Somebody stole my Bullet!" Frankie yelled.

Tom started to walk away. "I'll go get Uncle Mark," he said over his shoulder.

"You will do no such thing," Mamma said.

Tom turned around. "But if somebody stole Bullet," he said, "it is Uncle Mark's job to find the thief."

"We don't want to make any trouble for some little boy if he just took the rocking horse to play with it," Mamma said. "You and John D. see if you can find it before we ask for your uncle's help."

Tom and I went to Smith's vacant lot. There were about twenty kids there. Tom told them somebody had stolen Bullet. He made each one of them give his word of honor that he hadn't taken the rocking horse. Then he sent them to round up the rest of the kids in town and bring them to our barn. It was noon before Tom had finished questioning every kid in town and making him give his word of honor he hadn't taken Bullet. The only kid he didn't question was Paul Miller, who had the measles.

Mamma told Papa about the missing rocking horse during lunch. Frankie sat at the table red-eyed from crying and refused to eat.

"Some boy or a group of boys must have taken it," Papa said when Mamma finished.

"Impossible," Tom said. "I rounded up every kid in town and they all gave me their word that they didn't take it."

"I think," Mamma said, "it is time to turn the matter over to Mark."

Papa became goggle-eyed. "No," he said firmly. "It would make Mark the laughingstock of this town. Imagine a marshal and deputy sheriff looking for a stolen rocking horse. I

21

can just see people stopping him on the street and asking him if he's caught the rocking horse thief yet."

"But there must be something we can do," Mamma said. "Look at Frankie. He is so heartbroken that he can't eat."

"Now don't worry, son," Papa said to Frankie. "If your rocking horse doesn't turn up in a couple of days I'll buy you a new one."

"Don't want another one," Frankie cried. "I want Bullet."

Tom leaned forward. "Maybe if you offered a reward," he suggested to Papa.

"What you really mean," Papa said, "is that if I offer a reward you will put your great brain to work on solving the mystery. All right. That rocking horse cost over five dollars including shipping charges. You find Bullet within the next couple of days and I'll give you a dollar."

"I would try to find it anyway," Tom said, "because I love Frankie. What I was thinking is that some kid might have lied to me and a reward with no questions asked might get the rocking horse back."

After lunch Tom and I went to Smith's vacant lot, where Tom let the kids know there was a dollar reward with no questions asked for the return of Bullet. Again the fellows denied they had taken the rocking horse. We went home and Tom went up to his loft to put his great brain to work on the mystery. It was almost an hour before he came down.

"Did your great brain figure out what happened to Bullet?" I asked.

"Maybe," he said. "But I've got to talk to Uncle Mark."

"Papa said not to," I reminded him.

"I just want to ask him some questions," Tom said.

Uncle Mark was sitting at his desk. The three cells behind him were empty. Tom told him about the missing rocking horse.

"I'm sure," Tom continued, "that no kid in town took the rocking horse. They all gave me their word and nobody changed it when I offered a dollar reward with no questions asked. And besides, nobody would try to steal the rocking horse off our porch while Papa, Mamma, and Aunt Bertha were in our parlor. It was taken after they went to bed and by that time every kid in town was already in bed."

Uncle Mark leaned back in his chair. "Are you suggesting some grown man stole the rocking horse?" he asked.

"Yes," Tom said. "Were there many cowboys in town last night?"

"Not many on Friday nights," Uncle Mark said. "Saturday is their night to howl."

"What I was thinking," Tom said, "is that maybe a couple of cowboys who were drunk were riding down Main Street and took the rocking horse back to their ranch with them as a sort of joke. Remember the time those drunken cowboys stole the wooden horse in front of Jerry Stout's harness-and-saddle shop and took it all the way back to the Lazy Y Ranch with them?"

"It is possible," Uncle Mark said, "but I doubt it. The only cowboys in town last night were from ranches east and south of town. None of them would pass your house. And I saw them all ride out of town after the saloons closed."

"That eliminates cowboys and kids," Tom said. "Thanks, Uncle Mark."

"Do your mother and father want me to look into it?" Uncle Mark asked. And boy, oh, boy, did he look relieved when Tom said No. We left the marshal's office and began walking down Main Street.

23

"Where are we going?" I asked.

"Mrs. Higgins is always complaining to Mamma and everybody else about her insomnia," Tom said. "I hope she had it last night."

"You mean Mrs. Higgins stole the rocking horse because she can't sleep at night?" I asked, wondering why she would do such a thing.

"Don't be silly," Tom said. "My great brain tells me that nobody living in town stole the rocking horse. That means it must have been somebody from out of town."

"I see," I said. "You think Mrs. Higgins couldn't sleep and may have seen who took the rocking horse."

"Shucks no," Tom said as if digusted with me. "You know what a busybody Mrs. Higgins is. If she saw somebody stealing Bullet she would have screamed bloody murder and awakened everybody on the block."

"Then why do you want to talk to her?" I asked.

"If you will just shut up and keep your ears open you will soon find out," Tom answered.

Mrs. Higgins lived across the street from our house. She was a widow, who said she developed insomnia after her husband died. She was sitting in her parlor looking out the front bay window as she often did, so she saw us coming and had the front door open when we reached the porch.

"Hello, Thomas and John," she said. "Does your mother want to borrow some sugar or eggs or something?"

"No, Ma'am," Tom said. "Is your insomnia still bothering you, Mrs. Higgins?"

"It is getting worse all the time," she complained.

"Did it keep you awake last night?" Tom asked.

"It certainly did," she said. "I doubt if I got more than forty winks all night."

24

"You know how quiet it is around here at night except for a dog barking now and then," Tom said. "Did you hear anything that sounded like a horse or buggy or wagon on the street late last night?"

"That I did," she said. "It was after midnight. I distinctly heard the sound of wagon wheels on the gravel street. You know the sort of screeching sound wheels make on gravel. And I couldn't help wondering who was driving down the street at that time of night. I was going to get up and look but then the sound stopped."

Tom got an excited look on his freckled face. "You say the sound stopped as if the wagon had stopped," he said. "Did you hear it again?"

"Yes," Mrs. Higgins said. "It couldn't have been more than a couple of minutes before I heard the sound again. This time I got up. But when I looked out the parlor window the wagon was gone. And now, Thomas, why all these questions?"

"Because somebody stole Frankie's rocking horse off our front porch last night," Tom answered.

"Oh, the poor boy," Mrs. Higgins said. "And I did so enjoy sitting in my parlor and watching him playing cowboy on his rocking horse. Do you think whoever stopped the wagon last night stole the rocking horse?"

"I do," Tom said, "and now I've got to find out who it was. Thank you very much, Mrs. Higgins."

I thought we were going home when we left Mrs. Higgins, but Tom began walking toward the business district.

"Where are we going now?" I asked.

"Somebody driving a team and wagon stole Bullet," Tom said. "And that somebody doesn't live in Adenville. Now, why do people come to town with a wagon? To buy supplies.

That makes our next stop the Z. C. M. I. store."

Mr. Harmon was waiting on a customer when we entered. Tom waited until the customer had left.

"Mr. Harmon," he said, "do you remember anybody who drove into town in a team and wagon yesterday?"

"There were several who bought supplies from me," he said.

"Remember any of them who have a son or a daughter between the ages of, say, three and six?" Tom asked.

"Reckon you mean the Gruber family," Mr. Harmon said. "They have a son about four."

"I know who you mean," Tom said. "I've seen them in town several times. Are they very poor, Mr. Harmon?"

"Yes," Mr. Harmon said. "They own a small dry farm about six miles from town. That last drought really hurt them. Another dry spell and it will just about wipe them out. You've got to have rain to make money dry farming."

"Thank you very much, Mr. Harmon," Tom said.

We left the store and stood outside.

"Why do they call them dry farms?" I asked.

"Because they have no irrigation water," Tom said. "They depend on rain alone for their crops."

"Do you think the Grubers stole Bullet?" I asked.

"It all depends on whether they went back to their farm after buying supplies or stayed in town until after midnight," Tom said.

"How are you going to find that out?" I asked.

"Where is the one place in town a man could go with his team and wagon and family and not attract any attention?" Tom asked. "It would have to be the campgrounds. Let's get our bikes and ride over there."

When we arrived at the campgrounds there was only one family and two trappers camped there. Tom went over to the trappers who were sitting on boxes in front of their tent.

"Excuse me," Tom said, "but did you see a man with a black beard stop here yesterday? His wife and four-year-old son were with him."

One of the trappers with a tobacco-stained moustache spat out some tobacco juice. "We sure did, son," he said.

"What time did they leave?" Tom asked.

"Funny thing 'bout that," the man said. "Pete here and me was wonderin' why anybody would pull out in the middle of the night instead of waiting for daylight. We were just coming back after the saloons closed at midnight when we saw them leaving."

"Thank you," Tom said.

By the time we got home it was time to start doing the evening chores. I called Tom to one side in our backyard so Frankie couldn't hear.

"What are you going to do?" I asked. "If Mr. Gruber is too poor to buy a rocking horse and stole Bullet to give to his son maybe we'd better forget the whole thing. Papa can buy Frankie a new rocking horse."

Tom stared at me as if I had a carrot for a nose and a cabbage for a head. "That would mean forgetting about the dollar reward," he said. "I'm positive Mr. Gruber stole the rocking horse. He waited at the campgrounds until he knew everybody in our house would be asleep in bed and came here and stole Bullet. It was his wagon Mrs. Higgins heard. And I'm going to collect the reward."

Tom waited until after the supper dishes were washed and we were all in the parlor.

"Papa," he said, "my great brain has figured out who stole Bullet, but we will have to go to the Gruber farm to prove it."

Papa looked surprised. "I've known Jeb Gruber for years," he said. "He is an honest and hard-working man and not a thief."

"All the evidence points to him," Tom said. Then he explained how his great brain had solved the mystery.

Papa was shaking his head when Tom finished. "That is all very flimsy circumstantial evidence," he said.

Mamma leaned forward in her rocking chair. "Not so flimsy considering what I saw yesterday," she said. "I was washing the parlor window when I saw the Grubers. When their little boy spotted the rocking horse on our front porch he began clapping his hands and I could hear him shouting, 'Horsey!' Mr. Gruber stopped the team and wagon so the boy could get a good look at the rocking horse. Then they drove on down the street."

"I just can't believe that a man like Jeb Gruber would steal anything," Papa said.

"There is only one way to find out," Mamma said. "Frankie loves that rocking horse. I'm not asking you to have the man arrested if he did steal it. I just want you to get it back. It is a question of Frankie's happiness or the Gruber boy's happiness."

Frankie, who had been listening, got up from the floor where we were playing checkers. He walked over and put a hand on Papa's knee.

"Please, Papa," he pleaded. "Please get Bullet back for me. Please."

"All right, son," Papa said. "We'll drive out to the Gruber farm tomorrow."

We hitched our team to our buggy after Sunday dinner. Frankie rode with Papa in the front seat and Tom and I sat on the rear seat. As we rode towards the Gruber farm the evidence of the drought was all around us. The ground was so parched it was caked with withered crops lying in the sun. The Gruber farm was about a mile off the main highway. As we approached the farmhouse Frankie pointed toward it.

"Bullet!" he shouted happily.

And sure enough, on the front porch of the farmhouse we could see a little dark-haired boy riding the rocking horse. He didn't pay any attention to us. He was lost in his imagination. We could hear him shouting, "Giddy-up, Horsey!" Papa pulled the team to a halt as Mr. and Mrs. Gruber came out of the farmhouse and walked up to the buggy.

Mr. Gruber scratched nervously at his beard. "I know why you are here, Mr. Fitzgerald," he said. "Reckon as how somebody saw me do it. Thanks for not bringin' the sheriff."

Frankie grabbed Papa's hand as we got out of the buggy. "Let's get Bullet!" he shouted, but Papa held him firmly by the hand.

Mrs. Gruber brushed a strand of hair from her forehead. "I'm as much to blame as Jeb," she said. "I didn't try to stop him."

Papa looked at both of them. "I just don't understand *why* you took the rocking horse," he said.

"Our son Jimmy has diabetes," Mr. Gruber said. "About six months ago he started saying he was thirsty all the time and he drank a lot of water. My wife and I got worried when this went on for a couple of weeks and we took him to see

29

Doc LeRoy. Doc said Jimmy has diabetes. Ain't no cure for the disease. Doc said Jimmy had about two years to live."

Papa shook his head sadly.

"Friday when we went into town for supplies," Mr. Gruber continued, "Jimmy saw the rocking horse on the front porch of your house. He asked me if he could have a rocking horse like that. I couldn't afford to buy him one, but I wanted to make Jimmy happy. I said to Emma, 'I've got to get that rocking horse.' "

Mrs. Gruber nodded. "And I let him do it," she said.

"Reckon as how there is no more to say," Mr. Gruber said, "I'll fetch the rocking horse and put it in your buggy. And thanks again for not bringing the sheriff."

Papa picked Frankie up in his arms. "Do you understand why Mr. Gruber took Bullet?" he asked.

"Yes, Papa," Frankie said. "Jimmy is going to die."

"I'm going to leave it up to you, son," Papa said.

Papa put Frankie down. Frankie walked over to the front porch of the farmhouse. Jimmy Gruber was smiling happily as he rocked back and forth, but he stopped when Frankie got in front of him. Frankie just stared at Jimmy for a moment. Then he reached out and patted the head of the rocking horse.

"His name is Bullet," he said. "Please take good care of him." Then he ran to our buggy and climbed into the front seat.

Mr. Gruber blew his nose. "Just ain't no way to thank you and your boy enough," he said to Papa.

"It was worth a hundred rocking horses to see what Frankie just did," Papa said. "We'll be leaving now."

We walked to the buggy. Papa got into the front seat

with Frankie. Tom and I got in the back seat.

"I'm very proud of you, son," Papa said to Frankie as he started the team.

I looked back as Papa drove the team out of the farm-yard. I could see Jimmy Gruber riding the rocking horse while his parents watched him. I knew Frankie had done a very kind and generous thing. I knew I should feel glad about it. Instead I felt like crying. Maybe it was because a little four-year-old boy had less than two years to live. Then Tom interrupted my thoughts.

"What is diabetes, Papa?" he asked.

"I asked Dr. LeRoy about it when Ben Horner died from the disease a few years ago," Papa said. "He told me that the medical profession doesn't know what causes it and that's why they can't find a cure. All they know is that an adult will die from it within five years and a child will die within two years."

"What makes them die?" Tom asked.

"They don't get the benefit of the food they eat," Papa said, "because of changes the disease makes in their bodies, and eventually they go into a diabetic coma and die. But someday science will find a cure."

We didn't talk much during the rest of the drive home. Papa helped us unhitch the team and told Tom and me to give the horses a rubdown before doing the evening chores. Then he took Frankie by the hand.

"Let's go now, son," he said, "and put in an order to Sears Roebuck for a new rocking horse for you."

Tom stepped in front of them. "Aren't you forgetting something, Papa?" he asked. "I mean the reward."

"Good Lord," Papa said. "How can you think of money at a time like this?"

32

"You always said people should pay their debts promptly," Tom said. "And in a way the reward is a debt you owe me."

Papa removed his wallet from his pocket and took out a silver dollar which he handed to Tom. "There are times," he said, "when I think you have a cash register for a heart."

Tom watched Papa and Frankie leave the barn. "I wonder what's eating Papa," he said as he flipped the dollar up and down. "If my great brain hadn't solved the mystery of the missing rocking horse, Papa could have bought Frankie ten new rocking horses and none of them would have taken the place of Bullet in Frankie's heart. But knowing he has made Jimmy happy, Frankie will now be satisfied with a new rocking horse. Instead of being angry with me, Papa should be proud of me."

"Even my little brain can figure out why Papa is angry," I said. "Frankie sacrificed Bullet to make a little boy happy, but you still demanded the dollar reward."

Then Tom got angry. He held out the dollar towards me.

"If you don't think I earned this dollar, go ahead and take it," he dared me. "Just don't forget that if it hadn't been for me, every time Mr. and Mrs. Gruber looked at that rocking horse their consciences would have bothered them."

I had to admit it was worth more than a dollar not to have a guilty conscience.

"I guess you earned the dollar," I said.

"No guessing about it," Tom said as he put the dollar in his pocket. "You know darn well I earned it and so does Papa."

Jimmy Gruber lived for fifteen months after Frankie gave him the rocking horse. Papa was wrong about science discovering a cure for diabetes. Even today there is no cure. But in 1923 it was discovered that insulin and a controlled diet allowed diabetics to live as long as normal people.

CHAPTER THREE

The Horse Race

IT WAS SOON AFTER Jimmy Gruber's funeral that Howard Kay, who was one of my best friends, had a birthday party. Howard's party was held after school on a Friday. Mamma told Tom and Frankie they would have to do all the evening chores because I was going to the party. It was a sort of strange birthday party. We ate our fill of ice cream and cake all right but we didn't play any games like Pin-the-Tail-on-the-Donkey. The reason for this was that Howard's uncle, who owned a ranch, had given Howard a mare for a birthday present. We spent most of our time in the Kay barn admiring and petting the mare.

Howard was one of the very few kids in Adenville who

had a horse of his own when he was only six years old. His uncle had given him a saddle horse then named Blackie who was now getting pretty old. The time had come for Blackie to be turned out to pasture on the ranch and that is why Howard's uncle had given him the mare. She was a beauty. She had a light-brown coat and white forelegs and her face was all white down to her nose. Her name was Cleo and every kid at the party including me wished he had an uncle like Howard's.

The next morning after chores I told Tom and Frankie that I was going to the fairgrounds.

"Why the fairgrounds?" Tom asked.

"Didn't I tell you?" I said. "Howard is going to race his new mare against Parley Benson's pony Blaze."

"I hope that Howard wasn't stupid enough to bet," Tom said. "Blaze is the fastest quarter horse in the county."

"Cleo is a quarter horse too," I said. "They aren't going to bet. Howard just wants to find out how fast Cleo can run."

Frankie touched Tom on the arm. "What is a quarter horse?" he asked. "How can you have just a piece of a horse?"

Tom laughed. "It's a breed of horse that can run very fast for a short distance," he explained.

"But why do they call them quarter horses?" Frankie asked.

"Because the best distance they race is a quarter of a mile," Tom said. "They can beat any other kind of horse in a short race."

Tom and I got our bikes. Frankie rode double with Tom to the fairgrounds. Adenville was the county seat and every September the County Fair was held there. There was a grandstand for spectators. One big building was where the livestock were judged. Another building had booths in it where vegetables, prepared foods, and sewing were judged. Judges awarded blue ribbons to the best ear of corn, the best squash, and the best other vegetables. They also awarded a blue ribbon to the best needlepoint sewing, the best crocheting, the best homemade quilt, and things like that. Cakes, pies, homemade jams and jellies and other prepared foods were judged too and awarded ribbons.

Mamma usually won the first prize for the best fruitcake, but I think she cheated a little bit. She always put a little of Papa's brandy in her fruitcake mix. The Mormons never drank any alcoholic beverage and wouldn't know what it tasted like. I always figured it was the extra flavor the brandy gave Mamma's fruitcakes that made the judges award her first prize.

Next to the grandstand were chutes for the rodeo part of the fair. Each cowboy had to put up five dollars each time he entered a contest, and the winner got all the money. We had bronco-busting, bulldogging, calf-roping, and other contests. We had a quarter-mile horse race, too, which Parley had won two years in a row. But my favorite race was the race of the chuck wagons. The chuck-wagon cooks from different ranches drove their teams at a gallop with the wagons so close together that the hubs of their wheels were just inches apart.

There were about twenty kids in front of the grandstand when we arrived. Parley was sitting on Blaze. Howard rode up on his mare a few minutes later. He and Parley dismounted. Parley was too old to be invited to Howard's party and was seeing the mare for the first time.

"She looks a lot better than some of the quarter horses

I beat at the fair," Parley said.

"I know I can't beat you," Howard said. "I just want to find out how fast Cleo can run. I wish we had a stopwatch."

"We don't need one," Parley said. "We'll just see if I beat you by a greater distance than I did some of the horses at the fair."

Parley got on Blaze and Howard on Cleo. They asked Tom to act as starter. They took their places opposite the starting pole.

"I'll count to three," Tom said. "One, two, three, go!"

Howard's mare surprised me. She ran neck and neck with Blaze almost halfway around the quarter-mile racetrack. Then she began dropping back. Parley crossed the finish line about ten lengths in front of Cleo.

"Don't feel bad," Parley said to Howard when the race was over. "I beat four horses in the fair race by twenty lengths and I beat the other three by more than five lengths, so Cleo is faster than four of those quarter horses. Blaze is the fastest quarter horse in the whole county."

I knew Tom had something on his mind when we got home because he went straight up to his loft in the barn. He only went there when he was going to put his great brain to work on some scheme or swindle. He didn't come down until it was time for lunch.

"What were you doing in your loft?" I asked.

"Yeah, what?" Frankie said.

"That Parley sure likes to brag about his horse," Tom said.

"For my money," I said, "he has something to brag about."

"I can't stand a fellow who brags," Tom said.

38

"Boy, oh, boy," I said, "then you sure must hate yourself. You are always bragging about your great brain."

"That is different," Tom said.

I couldn't see any difference. But I did know that Tom had put his great brain to work on how to stop Parley from bragging about Blaze.

"If you're thinking of a way to beat Blaze in a race," I said, "forget it."

Tom nodded. "Yeah," he said, "but just think of how much money I could make betting if my great brain figured out a way to beat Blaze."

That evening Tom sat on the floor in the parlor with Frankie and me playing dominoes. I knew he didn't have his mind on the game because I beat him twice and Frankie beat us once. Finally he told Papa what was on his mind.

"Papa, why do cowboys all use mustangs instead of quarter horses?"

"Because a mustang has twice the stamina of a quarter horse," Papa said after placing a magazine he was reading on his lap. "A cowboy can work a mustang all day at hard labor that a quarter horse could never do. About the only thing a quarter horse is good for is as a saddle horse for pleasure riding or racing."

"Could a mustang outrun a quarter horse in a long race?" Tom asked.

"Definitely," Papa said. "In a race of more than half a mile the mustang would win."

A big grin came over Tom's freckled face. "Thanks, Papa," he said, and then proceeded to beat Frankie and me at dominoes until it was time to take our baths.

The next day after Sunday dinner Tom went up to our bedroom and changed to his playclothes.

"Where are you going?" I asked.

"To try an experiment," he answered.

"Can I come?" I asked.

"If you promise to keep your mouth shut about it," Tom said.

Eddie Huddle came over to play with Frankie. I went to the barn with Tom and helped him saddle up Sweyn's mustang Dusty. We rode to the fairgrounds. I got off. Tom stayed on Dusty.

"I'm going to see if Dusty can run a mile," he told me. "You watch and see if he slows down after I put him into a steady gallop."

I watched Tom ride Dusty around the track four times. Dusty was going just as fast the last time around as he had been going the first time. When they stopped, Dusty was breathing a little heavy but looked as if he could run around the track ten more times if he wanted to.

"I've got Parley where I want him," Tom said. "I'm going to challenge him to a race, Dusty against Blaze."

"Dusty hasn't got a chance," I said. "Blaze can run a lot faster."

"For a quarter of a mile, yes," Tom said, "and maybe even for half a mile. But this is going to be a mile-long race."

"But won't Parley know he can't beat Dusty in a mile-long race?" I asked.

"Parley is so proud of Blaze that he would bet on any kind of a race," Tom said. "To him Blaze is a racehorse and Dusty just an old mustang."

Monday after school we changed to our playclothes and went to Smith's vacant lot. Parley was there with about a dozen other kids.

"That was some race Saturday," Tom said as the fellows crowded around us.

"Blaze is the fastest horse in the county," Parley said. "Ain't one horse around here that can beat him."

"Maybe not in a quarter-of-a-mile race," Tom said. "But I don't believe Blaze could run a mile, let alone win a mile-long race."

Parley pushed his coonskin cap to the back of his head. "Blaze wasn't even puffing after he beat Cleo Saturday," he said. "A quarter of a mile is just exercise for him."

"I'd be willing to bet," Tom said, "that Sweyn's mustang Dusty can beat Blaze in a mile-long race."

"That old crowbait," Parley said disdainfully. "He must be nine or ten years old."

"He is eight years old," Tom said. "And I'll bet that 'old crowbait,' as you call him, can beat your Blaze in a mile-long race anytime."

"How much do you want to bet?" Parley asked, smiling confidently. "And when do you want to race?"

"Bet whatever you want," Tom said, "and that goes for the rest of you fellows. We'll race next Saturday morning after chores. Now let's forget about horse racing and play some scrub football."

Tom gave Dusty a double helping of oats that evening. He also gave him a double helping for the next four days. And every day after school he went to the fairgrounds and raced Dusty around the track four times to get him in shape for the race.

Saturday morning there were a couple dozen kids waiting at the fairgrounds when we arrived riding Dusty double. We dismounted. Tom handed me a paper sack. He took a notebook and pencil from his pocket.

"You fellows who want to bet line up," Tom said. "I'll write down your names and the amount of the bet. Put your money in the sack and I'll cover it with money from my pocket. I'm betting Dusty can beat Blaze in a mile-long race, which is four times around the track."

Tom was the only one who believed it, including me. The fellows got in line. Tom took and covered all their bets, from a nickel to half a dollar which Parley bet. Most of the kids bet a quarter. I knew there was close to ten dollars in the paper bag after all bets were made and Tom had covered them. Tom handed me the notebook and pencil.

"Danny, you act as starter," he said.

Tom got on Dusty and Parley on Blaze. They lined up at the starting pole. Danny counted to three and the race was on. Blaze pulled away from Dusty after only about a hundred feet. When Blaze finished the first lap, Dusty was only halfway around going at a steady gallop. The kids cheered Parley as he passed. I couldn't help feeling sorry for Tom.

On the second lap Tom was still behind about a third of the distance around the track. But on the third lap he began to gain and was only a few hundred feet behind as they passed the starting pole. I could see Blaze was tiring and slowing down, but he was still game. Tom passed Parley on Blaze at the halfway mark in the fourth lap. Dusty was running at that same steady gallop but Blaze had slowed down and was fall-

42

ing behind. Parley knew he was beaten when he hit the stretch with Tom about ten lengths in front of him. He used his quirt but Tom won the race by more than thirty lengths.

Tom stopped Dusty after crossing the finishing line. He jumped off and patted the mustang on the neck. Dusty was puffing but not too hard. Tom walked over and took the bag of money from me. Parley rode up on Blaze and dismounted. The quarter horse was heaving and was covered with lather and sweat.

"What do you think of this old crowbait now?" Tom asked, grinning.

Parley shook his head. "I should have known better than to bet you fifty cents," he said. "Pa has often said a mustang can run any other horse into the ground."

Danny Forester pushed his way up in front of Parley. "You told us to bet on you because you knew you couldn't lose," he said.

Then a rather strange thing took place. The kids who had lost money betting all crowded around Parley and blamed him. I say strange because usually when Tom won a bet they all crowded around him accusing him of swindling them or something.

"Know something, J. D.?" Tom said to me. "Seeing the fellows arguing with Parley has given me an idea."

He walked over to the group. "I don't blame you fellows for being angry at Parley," he said. "He should have won the race."

All the kids looked flabbergasted. Parley was the first to speak.

"The only way I could have won the race," he said, "would have been if Dusty had broken a leg."

44

"I don't know about that," Tom said. "I'd be willing to bet that I could beat you with me riding Blaze and you riding Dusty. It will give you and the other fellows a chance to win back the money you lost."

Parley looked angry. "What is this, a joke?" he demanded.

"No joke," Tom said. "We'll give both horses a rest until two o'clock this afternoon. Then I'll take all bets."

"Oh, no, you don't," Parley said. "You'll take Dusty home and fill him so full of oats and hay and water he won't be able to run."

"You can take Dusty home with you," Tom said, "and I'll take Blaze with me. Any of you fellows who want to bet be here at two o'clock."

I figured Tom's great brain had blown a fuse. There was no way Blaze could beat Dusty in a mile-long race.

"You are a fool," I said as we rode Blaze home.

"You sound as if you don't believe Blaze can beat Dusty in a mile race," Tom said.

"I just got through seeing that he couldn't," I said.

"Then put your money where your mouth is," Tom said.

I figured Tom had suddenly come down with brain fever or something. It was a golden opportunity to get even for some of the bets I'd lost to him.

"Bet you half a dollar," I said.

"It's a bet," Tom said.

It looked as if every kid in town was at the fairgrounds when we arrived that afternoon. Tom handed me a paper bag and got out his notebook and pencil.

"Line up," he said. "I'm betting that Blaze can beat

Dusty in a mile-long race with me riding Blaze and Parley riding Dusty."

Tom had plenty of takers. Kids who had only bet a nickel that morning now bet a dime. Kids who had bet a dime now bet a quarter. And kids who had bet a quarter now bet half a dollar. I knew there had to be more than fifteen dollars in the paper bag after the last bet was made.

Danny acted as starter. It was the same race we had seen that morning on the first lap around the track. Tom passed the starting pole while Parley on Dusty was only halfway around the track. But right then it became a different race. Tom slowed Blaze down to a walk and just let the horse walk and get its wind until Parley caught up with them. Then Tom laid the quirt on Blaze. Parley was a third of the way behind on the second lap. Again Tom slowed Blaze to a walk and waited for Parley to catch up. Then around they went again. This time Parley was behind about one-fourth of the way around the track when Tom passed the starting pole. Again Tom slowed Blaze down to a walk. This time he not only waited until Parley caught up with him, he let Parley get a few hundred feet in front before he gave Blaze the quirt. He overtook Parley when they reached the stretch. Both horses came thundering down the stretch with Blaze slowly pulling ahead. Blaze wasn't running as fast as the first times around the track but he was going fast enough to win the race by about five lengths. But did the fellows think Tom had won fair and square? Heck no.

Parley jumped off Dusty. "You cheated," he shouted. "You slowed Blaze down to a walk after each lap and let him get his wind again."

Danny nodded. "Parley is right," he said. "In a horse race

a horse is supposed to run, not walk."

"Hold it on that cheating stuff," Tom said, "or somebody is going to get a bloody nose and a black eye. The bet was that I could beat Parley in a mile race. Both horses covered the distance of a mile and I won the race. If Parley had done what I did this morning he would have won. And I'll bet you fellows wouldn't have said anything about cheating then."

I could tell from the looks on the fellows' faces that they knew Tom was right. They all went home sadder and poorer. I rode double on Dusty with Tom to our barn. He put the bag of coins on a bale of hay. We unsaddled Dusty and gave the mustang a good rubdown. Then Tom sat down on the bale of hay and counted the money in the bag. He had a big grin on his face when he finished. Counting the money he had won that morning, he had taken the fellows for more than thirteen dollars. But did that satisfy him? Heck no.

"Before we start doing the evening chores," he said, "let's go up to our bedroom so you can get that half-dollar you owe me."

"I know one thing for sure," I said. "I hope I get typhoid fever and die if I ever make another bet with you."

"Papa and Mamma will see to it that you have a nice funeral," Tom said. "But, seriously, J. D., you should be grateful that I keep winning bets from you."

"What's there to be grateful for about me losing money to you?" I asked.

Tom put a hand on my shoulder. "I just bet you now and then to teach you a lesson so you won't turn out to be a gambling man," Tom said. "When I get through with you, you will never bet or gamble."

"And neither will any other kid in town," I said, "because they won't have any money to gamble with when they grow up. You'll have it all."

I don't know why that made Tom laugh. I didn't think it was funny at all. I meant every word of it.

CHAPTER FOUR

Tom and the Dude

WITH CHRISTMAS COMING UP Tom temporarily gave up his swindling ways after winning all that money on the horse race. My oldest brother, Sweyn, was coming home for the Christmas holidays. We all went down to the depot to meet him.

When Sweyn left to go back east for his first year of high school, he was wearing a blue serge worsted suit with knee-length britches and a cap like all boys in Adenville wore until they were sixteen. A fellow didn't get a pair of long pants until he was sixteen. But when Sweyn, who was only fifteen, returned home, he had blossomed out into a full-blown dude. He was wearing a light-gray checkered cassimere wool suit with long pants, shoes without laces that you pulled on, a derby hat, a blue-and-white striped corded front shirt, a purple necktie with a handkerchief to match in the breast pocket of the suit, and silk embroidered suspenders, all the likes of which had never been seen in Adenville, and maybe not even in all of Utah.

You can bet that Tom, Frankie, and I held our heads down with shame as we walked towards home. People on the street turned around to stare at my oldest brother, peeked out of windows, and came out of stores to watch. It was a sight never seen before in Adenville, a full-blown dude walking down Main Street. I had never felt so humiliated in my life.

Sweyn had arrived on the eleven o'clock morning train on Monday, December the 19th. He would be home for ten days. Boy, oh, boy, the thought of having the fellows see my big sissy dude brother with his fancy duds for ten days was enough to make me want to run away from home. It was bad enough when Sweyn had disgraced us by starting to go with a girl at the age of thirteen. And now at the age of fifteen he had turned into a real sissy dude.

Sweyn was in such a hurry to show off his fancy duds to his girl, Marie Vinson, that he excused himself from the table as soon as we finished lunch. He got his derby hat from the hallway hat rack and came back into the dining room.

"*Adieu* and toodle-oo," he said with a wave of the derby.

Tom stood up. "And a cockle-doodle-doo to you," he said, flapping his arms as if they were the wings of a rooster.

That made everybody but Sweyn laugh.

"*Enfant,*" he said and then left.

Tom sat back down at the table and looked at Papa. "What is that 'adieu,' 'toodle-oo,' and 'enfant' business?" he asked.

"Your brother is just showing off some of the French he learned during his first term in high school," Papa replied. "*Adieu* means goodbye and *enfant* is French for infant."

"I'll infant him," Tom said frowning. "And what about that 'toodle-oo'? What kind of an insult is that?"

"It isn't an insult," Papa said, chuckling. "It is a rather common expression back east like we say so long out west."

Tom shook his head. "Are you and Mamma going to let Sweyn run around Adenville wearing those fancy duds and giving people that 'adieu' and 'toodle-oo' business?"

"Why not?" Papa asked.

"I'll tell you why not," Tom said. "People will think he has turned into an eighteen-karat sissy for sure."

"Don't be too hard on your brother," Papa said. "It is a phase every boy goes through during his first year of high school."

"Not me," Tom said. "If I have to wear fancy duds like that to go to high school in Pennsylvania next year, I'm not going."

"You will change your mind when you get there," Papa said. "All things, including clothing, are relative to time and place."

"What do you mean by that?" Tom asked.

"Well," Papa said smiling, "I wouldn't walk down Main Street and go to work at the *Advocate* office wearing my nightshirt because it is the wrong time and place to wear a nightshirt. But it is perfectly proper to wear my nightshirt to bed because that is the time and place for it."

That made us all laugh.

"Seriously, T. D.," Papa said, "you would be just as much out of place wearing clothing suitable for Adenville at high school back in Boylestown, Pennsylvania, as your

51

brother is wearing his eastern clothing here in Adenville."

"Then why don't you make him stop wearing those fancy duds while he is home?" Tom asked.

"Let him enjoy himself by showing off his new wardrobe to his girl," Papa said.

"Maybe Sweyn will enjoy himself," Tom said, "but J. D., Frankie, and I sure won't. The fellows will really make fun of us for having a sissy dude for a brother."

After lunch Eddie Huddle came over to play with Frankie. I sat on the railing of our corral fence with Tom.

"Why are we sitting here?" I asked. "It's Christmas vacation. Let's go to Smith's vacant lot and play with the fellows."

"I don't feel like listening to the fellows rub salt in our wounds because we've got a sissy dude brother," Tom said. "I'm going up to my loft and put my great brain to work on how to make Sweyn stop wearing those fancy duds while he is home."

I didn't want to just sit on our corral fence for my Christmas vacation. I decided to heck with it and went to Smith's vacant lot. Tom was sure right. All the fellows stopped playing and crowded around me. Parley pushed his coonskin cap to the back of his head.

"Who was that fancy pants your family met at the train this morning?" he asked.

"You know darn well it was my brother Sweyn," I said.

Danny Forester grinned. "I'll bet he uses perfume," he said.

Seth Smith nodded. "And pomade on his hair," he said.

Hal Evans got in his licks. "If I had a sissy dude brother

like that," he said, "I'd go hide in the mountains and become a hermit."

Seth patted my shoulder. "I feel sorry for you and Tom," he said. "It must run in the family. That means both you and Tom will become sissies and dudes when you are fifteen."

"We will not," I said. "Tom is up in his loft right now putting his great brain to work on how to make Sweyn get rid of all those fancy duds."

I thought they would leave me alone after that but they didn't. They kept making disparaging remarks about Sweyn until I got disgusted and went home. I waited for Tom until he came down from his loft to help with the evening chores.

"Boy, oh, boy," I said. "You were sure right. The fellows let me have it with both barrels until I couldn't stand it anymore and came home. Did your great brain figure anything out yet?"

"Not yet," Tom said. "But it will. I'm not going to let Sweyn spoil our Christmas vacation."

"If your great brain doesn't do something," I said, "I'm going to pretend I'm sick and stay in bed for the whole Christmas vacation."

That evening Sweyn went up to his room. He didn't come down until Mamma and Aunt Bertha had finished the supper dishes. He had on a brand-new dude outfit. He was wearing white flannel trousers, a thing he called a blazer that was like a coat only it was made from light material that had big red and white stripes on it, and he was carrying a straw hat in one hand and a tennis racket in the other hand.

Tom stared at him bug-eyed. "Have you gone plumb loco?" he asked. "There aren't any tennis courts in Adenville and you can't play tennis in the dark anyway."

"I promised Marie that I'd show her my tennis outfit," Sweyn said. "And if I do say so myself, I learned to play a very good game of tennis back east. And next summer I'm going to get some young fellows together and build us a tennis court here in Adenville."

"But you can't go walking down Main Street in that out-fit," Tom said. "People will think you are crazy wearing white flannel trousers and a straw hat and carrying a tennis racket in the middle of winter."

"You're just jealous of my outfit," Sweyn said.

"How can I be jealous of a jackass?" Tom asked. Then he turned to Papa. "Please stop him. He'll make us the laugh-ingstock of Adenville."

But Papa just smiled. "I think you are making a moun-tain lion out of a kitten," he said.

Mamma agreed. "And so do I," she said. "And Sweyn D., you do look very nice."

Sweyn gave us a wave with his straw hat. "Toodle-oo, everybody," he said as he left.

Right on the spot I decided not to show my face out-side the house until Sweyn went back to high school. Some of the fellows were sure to see him and boy, oh, boy, would they rub it in. I continued playing checkers with Frankie, but he beat me because I didn't have my mind on the game. Tom was reading a book, but I knew his mind wasn't on what he was doing either. Then Mamma spoke.

"The ragbag is almost full, Bertha," she said. "I think we should start making another patch quilt."

Aunt Bertha looked up from the sock she was darning. "Can't start tomorrow," she said. "The Ladies Sewing Circle

54

meets, remember?"

"Of course," Mamma said. "It's Nellie Nelms's turn. But we will start the day after tomorrow on the quilt."

I was surprised to see how interested Tom had become in the conversation. He stopped reading and just sat there. I knew his great brain was working on something because of the furrows in his forehead.

I couldn't see why the ragbag would interest Tom. Mamma never threw anything away. When our clothes wore out she laundered them and put them in the ragbag in the bathroom closet. When she needed a rag she always took out something white, like a worn-out suit of underwear. All the colored pieces in the ragbag she kept to make patch quilts. I was so curious as to why the ragbag interested Tom that I stayed awake that night until he came up to bed.

"Why were you so interested in the ragbag?" I asked, sitting up in bed.

"My great brain has come up with a plan to make Sweyn stop wearing those fancy duds," Tom said. "We'll put the plan into action tomorrow afternoon when Mamma and Aunt Bertha leave for the Ladies Sewing Circle. Don't ask me any more questions. There are a few details my great brain has to figure out."

I was as curious as all get out, but I didn't learn any more until the next afternoon. I was sitting on the back porch steps with Tom and Frankie. Mamma opened the kitchen door. She was all dressed up.

"Bertha and I are leaving now," she said.

We walked to the side of the house and waited until we saw Mamma and Aunt Bertha going down the street.

"Everything is working out perfect," Tom said. "Mamma and Aunt Bertha are gone. Papa has Sweyn helping him at the *Advocate*. Let's go."

Tom got the ragbag and dumped its contents on the floor.

"What's the idea?" I asked.

"Yeah, what?" Frankie said.

"Sweyn's girl, Marie Vinson, has been at Saint Mary's Academy in Salt Lake City since school started," Tom said. "She hasn't seen any of us since last summer. Now do as I tell you and stop asking questions. Strip down to your underwear and take off your shoes and stockings."

Tom began looking through the pile of stuff from the ragbag. Mamma had a system. When we got a new suit it became our Sunday best, which we wore to church. When it became too worn for church we wore the suit to school. When it became too worn for school we wore the suit for playclothes, and it remained playclothes as long as Mamma could mend and patch it. Then it was fit only for the ragbag.

Tom picked out an old Buster Brown suit of Frankie's that was worn and patched. Then he picked out a worn-out suit for himself and one for me. He hunted until he found us all worn and patched shirts, and he tore a few of the patches off before he handed them to us. All the clothes were too small for us because we'd grown. When we got dressed we looked like three ragamuffins from the poorest family in town.

"Now here is the plan," Tom said. "I want Marie Vinson to think Papa and Mamma are spending so much money buying Sweyn fancy duds that the three of us have to wear rags. Let's go."

"But no kid goes barefooted this time of the year," I protested.

"I want her to think we don't even have stockings and shoes to wear," Tom said.

We sneaked down alleys without being seen until we were in back of the Vinson home.

"We know Mr. Vinson is at work," Tom said, "and Mrs. Vinson is at the Ladies Sewing Circle meeting. That means Marie must be alone in the house. Follow me."

He led us to the back porch and knocked on the kitchen door. A moment later Marie Vinson opened the door.

"We didn't want to disgrace you by going to the front door," Tom said. "But I've got to see my brother, Sweyn, and ask him if I can use his mustang, Dusty. Is he here?"

Marie stood bug-eyed and tongue-tied for about a minute before she could speak.

"You . . . you . . . you can't be," she finally said. "No, I know you are Sweyn's brothers. Why are you dressed like that? Are you going to a masquerade party?"

"No," Tom said, sadly shaking his head. "These are the clothes we wear to school and all the time now. You see, it has cost Papa and Mamma so much money to send Sweyn back east to school and buy him all those fancy clothes, there just isn't any money left to buy clothes for us."

"But that isn't fair," Marie said.

"Papa and Mamma can't help it," Tom said. "Sweyn is their pet. They give him everything he wants even if it means we have to wear rags. I guess he isn't here. I wonder where he could be?"

"He told me that he had to help your father at the *Advocate* this afternoon," Marie said.

"Thank you," Tom said. "I'll see him there."

"And when you do," Marie said, "just tell him that I never want to see him again, the selfish thing."

She shut the door. Tom winked at Frankie and me. We had a hard time not laughing until we reached the alley. Then we laughed all the way home. We put the old clothes back in the ragbag and got dressed in our regular clothes.

"She went for it hook, line, and sinker," Tom said grinning. "The first part of my great brain's plan was a complete success."

Frankie looked up at Tom. "But won't Sweyn be mad?" he asked.

"If my plan works," Tom said, "he will not only be angry but also heartbroken. We can't take a chance of Marie Vinson seeing us dressed like this. We'll have to play in our own backyard the rest of the day."

That evening after supper Sweyn got all dressed up in another new suit, new shirt, and new necktie. He sat in the parlor staring at the clock on the mantelpiece.

Papa noticed. "Calling on your girl again tonight?" he asked.

"At seven o'clock," Sweyn said.

"Time moves slowly for lovers when they are apart," Papa said.

That made Sweyn blush.

Mamma and Aunt Bertha finished the supper dishes and came into the parlor. Mamma looked at Sweyn.

"Aren't you going to spend one evening at home during your Christmas vacation?" she asked.

"I'll stay home Christmas Eve and Christmas night and of course the night before I go back east," Sweyn said.

Papa took a puff on his after-dinner cigar. "You'll do better than that," he said. "We do not mind sharing you with

Marie Vinson but we don't want her monopolizing all of your time. I think seeing her every other night is enough."

Sweyn looked as disappointed as a dog would if you took away its bone.

"All right, Dad," he said as he stood up. Then he gave us a wave of his derby hat and that 'toodle-oo' business and left.

About twenty minutes later Sweyn returned. Papa was reading a farm magazine. Aunt Bertha was knitting. Mamma was crocheting a doily. Tom was reading a book. Frankie and I were playing dominoes on the floor. We all stopped what we were doing and stared at Sweyn. He walked, no, he staggered, as if he were drunk, to a chair and slumped down in it. His face was pale. He looked positively sick.

"Are you ill?" Mamma asked.

Sweyn pressed his hand to his heart. "Only here," he said. "You won't have to worry about Marie monopolizing any more of my time."

Mamma was the first to speak. "What happened between you and Marie?" she asked.

"I rang the front doorbell," Sweyn said as if he were reading a funeral service over a grave. "She opened the door. She gave me a nasty look and said she never wanted to see me again because I was the most selfish person in the world."

"Selfish?" Mamma asked.

Sweyn nodded sadly. "That is what she called me just before she slammed the door in my face," he said.

"Are you sure she wasn't just teasing you?" Mamma asked. "Young girls do that you know."

"I'm sure," Sweyn said. "I rang the doorbell again. This

time her mother answered it. She told me that Marie never wanted to see me again. I just don't understand it. We've been going together since I was thirteen. We wrote to each other every week while she was at Saint Mary's Academy and I was in Boylestown. We had a sort of understanding that some day . . ." He didn't finish the sentence as he stood up. "I think I'll go up to my room," he said.

We watched him leave and heard him go upstairs to his room. Mamma looked very concerned.

"I'm going to phone Ida Vinson and find out what this is all about," she said.

I thought for sure Mamma was going to blow Tom's plan sky-high but Papa saved the day.

"People who interfere in young lovers' quarrels are asking for trouble," he said.

"But I don't understand the selfish part," Mamma said.

"I think I do," Papa said. "Sweyn had promised to go horseback riding with Marie this afternoon. He was quite upset when I told him I needed him at the *Advocate*. He phoned Marie from the office. And being so young I guess she considered it selfish of him not to keep his promise and go riding with her."

Later Tom surprised me by going upstairs with Frankie and me when it was our bedtime. He could stay up an hour later if he wanted.

"Now for the second part of my plan," Tom said. "You two wait here."

"No," I said. "We want to listen."

"All right," Tom said, "but take off your shoes."

Frankie and I took off our shoes. We followed Tom to

61

the door of Sweyn's bedroom. The transom was open. We could hear Sweyn sort of crying and groaning at the same time.

"Got him," Tom whispered.

Then he motioned for Frankie and me to stand on the side of the doorway so we wouldn't be seen when the door was opened. Tom knocked on the door.

"Just a minute," Sweyn called.

It was more than a minute before he opened the door. Tom entered the bedroom and closed the door behind him.

"I heard you crying," Tom said. "You really must be stuck on Marie Vinson."

Frankie and I could hear perfectly through the open transom.

"I know I'm only fifteen," Sweyn said, "but I've been in love with Marie for two years. And now it is all over. I think I'll run away to sea."

"It's too bad you aren't old enough to join the French Foreign Legion," Tom said. "But I guess you are old enough to become a cabin boy on a ship."

"I don't care what happens to me," Sweyn cried out. "Without Marie life has lost all meaning."

"You've really got it bad," Tom said. "I guess you would do just about anything to fix things like they were before to-night."

"I'll say I would," Sweyn said.

"Would you stop wearing all those fancy eastern duds and just wear your old blue serge suit until you go back to school?" Tom asked.

"What has the clothing I wear got to do with Marie?" Sweyn asked.

62

"Do you want my great brain to fix things between you and Marie or not?" Tom demanded.

"Sure, if you can," Sweyn said.

"I can," Tom said. "But first you will have to give me your word of honor you will never mention it to Papa or Mamma."

"I'm beginning to smell something," Sweyn said.

"Smell all you want," Tom said. "I came here to help you make up with your girl. But you don't want my help. So go back to your bawling and groaning."

"Wait," Sweyn said. "I'll do anything you say if you get me back my girl. I give you my word I won't say anything to Papa or Mamma."

"And will you also give me your word that you will stop wearing all those fancy duds you bought back east?" Tom asked.

"I don't know what my clothing has to do with it," Sweyn said, "but I give you my word."

"All right," Tom said. "Tomorrow morning after breakfast we'll straighten this whole thing out. And remember to wear your old blue serge suit with the knee britches."

The next morning Tom, Frankie, and I all got dressed in our Sunday best suits. Sweyn wore his old blue serge. Mamma was goggle-eyed when she saw us enter the kitchen for breakfast.

"Why are you three boys all dressed up?" she asked. "And Sweyn D., why are you wearing your old suit?"

"We'll do the chores later," Tom said. "But first we have to call on Marie Vinson and convince her that S. D. isn't a selfish person."

63

Papa wasn't fooled. "I have a feeling," he said to Tom, "that this is another one of your great brain schemes."

Sweyn spoke before Tom could. "I don't care what it is as long as Marie and I make up," he said.

After breakfast the four of us went to the Vinson home. Mrs. Vinson opened the front door.

"We must talk to Marie," Tom said.

"She is up in her room," Mrs. Vinson said. "I'll call her."

In a couple of minutes Marie came to the front door. She looked at Sweyn and then stared bug-eyed at Tom, Frankie, and me.

"I'm sorry," Tom said, "but we played a mean joke on you and Sweyn yesterday. We dug those old clothes out of our ragbag. We have plenty of clothes to wear. Our father is quite well off and can afford to send Sweyn back east to school and buy him the latest fashions in clothing."

"I don't understand," Marie said. "Why did you let me think you had to dress like ragamuffins because of Sweyn?"

"To make him stop wearing those fancy duds in Adenville," Tom said. "Being a girl maybe you won't understand. But all the fellows are making fun of J. D. and me because they say we've got a sissy dude for a brother. We will both be getting into fights every day as long as Sweyn wears those fancy clothes. Anyway, if you love him it won't make any difference what kind of clothes he wears."

Marie stepped out on the porch. She took hold of Sweyn's hand and smiled at him.

"I wouldn't care if you called on me wearing overalls," she said. "I cried all night."

"So did I," Sweyn said.

And that is how The Great Brain got rid of a dude. And for my money, if being in love can make you stay awake and cry all night, I hope I never fall in love.

CHAPTER FIVE

The Chute-the-Chute

WITH SWEYN NO LONGER WEARING his fancy duds to humiliate Tom, Frankie, and me, it turned out to be a happy Christmas except for one thing. It had never occurred to me until that year that the mere preparation for Christmas was almost as enjoyable as the holiday itself.

Sweyn, Tom, Frankie, and I all went with Papa in our buggy to the forest to get a Christmas tree. Papa finally picked a blue spruce that was just the right size. It was so beautiful I hated to see him and Sweyn cut it down. We placed the bottom of the tree trunk in a bucket in our parlor and wedged it with pieces of coal to hold the tree upright. Then we filled the bucket with water. Mamma covered the bucket with a white sheet and then the tree was ready to decorate. We didn't have fancy ornaments except for an angel that went on top of the tree. We used needles and thread to make strings of red cranberries and white popcorn to put on the tree. We put pieces of cotton on the branches to make it look like snow. We hung painted pinecones and red-striped candy canes on the tree. During the week before Christmas our big kitchen was filled with wonderful smells as Mamma and Aunt Bertha made candy, cookies, cakes and pies, and other goodies.

Frankie was six years old and still believed in Santa Claus. I guess he really did because he wanted Papa to clean our fireplace chimney so Santa wouldn't get his red and white suit dirty. Papa assured him that Santa used magic not to get soot on his suit. On Christmas Eve we hung our stockings on the mantelpiece knowing they would be filled with an orange, candy, and nuts in the morning. And we crowded around Mamma at the piano and sang Christmas carols until it was time to go to bed.

We never opened our presents until Christmas morning. I got the repeating air rifle that I wanted. Frankie got a new wagon. Tom received a wallet. Sweyn got a pair of cuff links with his initials on them. Mamma gave Papa a stickpin with a pearl on it. He gave her one of those watches that ladies pin to their blouses. We all gave Aunt Bertha a present. There were also presents from Aunt Cathie and Uncle Mark and from Boylestown, Pennsylvania, presents arrived from Uncle Harry and Aunt Mary Fitzgerald with whom Sweyn lived while going to high school.

Everything was perfect except the presents that Tom, Frankie, and I chipped in to buy for Papa and Mamma. We ordered a hat from an advertisement in a magazine that I thought was elegant for Mamma. It had an imitation bird's nest on top with an imitation canary in the nest. Mamma had always bought Papa neckties, which were plain colored or polka dots. We decided to give Papa a treat and bought him a beauty with big gold and blue stripes. Our parents were not only bug-eyed but tongue-tied when they saw the presents on Christmas morning.

That evening Mamma made all of us boys take a dose of castor oil because we'd eaten so much candy and sweets besides a turkey dinner. I woke up about ten o'clock and had to go downstairs to the bathroom. I got halfway down the stairway and stopped. I could hear Papa and Mamma talking in the parlor.

"I know the boys meant well," Papa said, "but I wouldn't wear that necktie to a dog fight. And as for that hat they bought you, only a dance hall girl from one of the saloons would wear a hat like that."

"I know, dear," Mamma said. "But you will wear the necktie and I'll wear the hat."

"But what will people say when they see us?" Papa asked.

"I don't care what people will say," Mamma said. "All I care about is not hurting the boys' feelings. They gave us the presents because they love us. We'll show how much we love them by wearing the necktie and the hat."

"You are right, of course," Papa said. "All we can hope for is that I spill some printer's ink on the tie and you get caught in a rainstorm and ruin the hat."

I sneaked back upstairs. Then I coughed as I came down the stairway. Mamma heard me and met me at the bottom of the stairs.

"Are you ill, John D.?" she asked.

"No, Mamma," I said. "I just have to go to the bathroom."

I sure felt awful about the necktie and hat. That was the one thing that went wrong with Christmas. I never did tell Tom and Frankie, figuring there was no sense in making them feel bad too. At the same time I couldn't help feeling grateful to Papa and Mamma for loving us enough to wear the necktie and the hat. And I didn't blame Papa when he spilled some printer's ink on the necktie the second time he wore it. And I guess Mamma knew it was going to rain the day she first wore the hat and ruined it.

The present that provided Tom with his next great brain's scheme to make money was the wagon Frankie got for Christmas. The holidays were over. Sweyn had gone back to school. It was the first Saturday after school started and Tom, Frankie, and I were sitting on the corral fence after finishing our chores.

"Buying all those Christmas presents has just about made a pauper out of me," Tom said.

Tom calling himself a pauper was like Mr. Thompson the butcher saying he didn't have any meat in his meat market.

"You wouldn't be satisfied if you were a millionaire," I said. "You are the wealthiest kid in town and have got more money than a lot of adults."

"Maybe so," Tom said, "but I haven't made any money since the horse race and that was a long time ago. And besides, there is nothing to do in this town when I haven't got a deal of some kind going for me."

"What do you mean nothing to do?" I asked. "We can play basketball, football, and baseball."

"I mean something exciting like the amusement park in Salt Lake City," Tom said. "When I was going to the Jesuit Catholic Academy, Father Rodrigues took all the students to this big amusement park one Saturday. They had everything there, a merry-go-round, a Ferris wheel, a roller coaster, and a chute-the-chute."

"I've seen pictures of a Ferris wheel and a roller coaster," I said, "but what is a chute-the-chute?"

"Yeah, what?" Frankie said.

"You get on a thing with wheels that looks like a coaster," Tom said, "and it goes way up high. Then it comes down the track lickety-split, so fast you think you are flying."

"Boy, oh, boy," I said. "I'd sure like to ride on a chute-the-chute."

"I'll bet a lot of kids would," Tom said. "And that gives me an idea. Frankie, you won't be using your old wagon now that you've got a new one. What do you want for it?"

"Why do you want it?" Frankie asked.

"To make a coaster for my chute-the-chute," Tom said. "All I want are the wheels and axles. Those axles are heavy iron and braced. The wheels have strong spokes and heavy welded steel rims. They are strong enough to take the jolt of coming off a chute-the-chute."

"What will you give me for them?" Frankie asked.

"Ten free rides on the chute-the-chute when it is finished," Tom answered.

"It's a deal," Frankie said.

"Hold it," I said. "Maybe you can make a coaster but how are you going to make the track for the chute-the-chute?"

"Out of that lumber left over from tearing down our icehouse," Tom answered.

Everybody had an icehouse of their own until that previous summer. They went or hired somebody to go to the frozen lakes in the mountains in the wintertime and cut cakes of ice. The cakes were about three feet long, two feet wide, and two feet deep. They were placed in rows in an icehouse and then covered with sawdust to stop them from melting during the summer. But last summer Hank Morgan built a big icehouse and went into the business of selling ice door to door with his ice wagon. It cost a little more but it was worth it. Our icehouse had lain vacant for a few months and then Papa had it taken down. We had been using the lumber for kindling wood but there was a lot of wood left.

"You had better ask Papa about it before you start building your chute-the-chute," I said. "He was saving that lumber for kindling wood."

"There will be plenty left," Tom said. "I'll make a track from the edge of our barn down to the ground where the icehouse used to be."

I can't say that Papa was enthusiastic about the idea when we went to the *Advocate* office to ask him.

"I don't know," he said. "It sounds rather dangerous to me."

"Let me build the track," Tom said, "and you can inspect it and the coaster before any kid rides the chute-the-chute. You always said it takes brains to make money and this is one of the best ideas my great brain ever had to make money. Besides, the kids in town will get a thrilling ride they would have had to go all the way to Salt Lake City to get."

"All right," Papa said. "But if I decide it isn't safe you will have to tear it down."

We left the *Advocate* office and stopped at the Z. C. M. I.

71

store. Tom had been so sure Papa would say yes that he'd brought along enough money to buy a pound of sixteen-penny nails, a hook, and fifty feet of quarter-inch rope.

"I'll need a box to make a coaster," Tom said.

"Help yourself to any you find out in back," Mr. Harmon said.

But there wasn't the right size wooden box in back of the store. Tom explained to Mr. Harmon the size of the box he needed. Mr. Harmon took us into the storeroom. Tom picked out a box. We helped Mr. Harmon empty the canned milk from it and put the cans on a shelf.

When we arrived in our barn Tom put his arm around my shoulders.

"Out of the goodness of my heart," he said, "I'm going to make you a ten-percent partner in this business venture of mine. I'll need you to help build the track and to pull the coaster back up after each ride."

"It's a deal," I said.

Tom removed the wheels and axles from Frankie's old wagon. He got a two-by-four from the old icehouse lumber and sawed off two pieces two feet long. He turned the box over and nailed the pieces of two-by-four on each end. Then he fastened the axles to the two pieces of lumber by driving nails in part way and then bending them over the axles. He used part of the lid of the box to make a seat in the coaster. Then he cut off a piece of the lid about two inches wide which he nailed near the front to be used as a hand railing. He sat down in the seat and grabbed the hand railing.

"This is how you ride the coaster," he said.

"But you can't steer it," I protested.

"You don't have to steer it," he said. "The track I'm going to build will make the coaster steer itself."

After eating lunch Tom began building the track for the chute-the-chute on the ground where the old icehouse had been.

"The track will be thirty-six feet long," he said. "First we'll pick out six twelve-foot two-by-fours."

Parley, Danny, and Seth arrived. Tom told them what he was doing. They offered to help for nothing. Tom laid out three two-by-fours flat. He joined them together with a two-foot brace. He did the same with the other three two-by-fours. Then he laid the two thirty-six foot pieces of track side by side. He got the coaster and got Danny and Parley to separate the two pieces of track so the wheels of the coaster fit on the track. Then he nailed a cross brace at each end and in the middle. Then he turned the track right side up. He pushed the coaster from one end to the other to make sure the wheels fit the track.

Parley pushed his coonskin cap to the back of his head. "The coaster will run off the track," he said.

"Not when we get through," Tom said. "We'll get six more twelve-foot two-by-fours and nail them to the sides of the track. That will leave two inches sticking up above where the wheels go and keep the coaster on the track.

When that was finished we lifted one end of the track to the edge of the barn. Tom got our long ladder. He climbed up to the roof and nailed the end brace through the shingles and sheathing. Then he came down to the ground.

"That will hold it to the roof," he said. "But my father said it must be one-hundred-percent safe. We'll dig two holes under the center of the track. Then we'll get two twelve-foot two-by-fours and stick them in the holes and tamp down the dirt good. Then I'll climb up the track and nail the two two-by-fours to each side of the track. That will make two solid braces from the ground to the track."

After that was finished Tom stood back to admire the track. "The cross braces will prevent the track from spreading," he said. "The underpinnings will make it solid enough for a man to ride in the coaster, let alone a boy. I'm going to give it a trial run."

"You can't do that," I said. "Papa must inspect the coaster and track first."

Tom looked plumb disgusted with me. "How will I know it's safe for Papa to inspect if I don't try it first?" he said.

We got the coaster from the barn and the fifty-foot rope. Tom fastened the hook he had bought to the rear of the coaster.

"Now, J. D.," he said, "climb up on the barn and brace your feet against the brace on the track."

I did as I was told while Tom made a loop on one end of the rope and fastened it to the hook on the coaster. Then he threw the rest of the rope up to me. I caught it.

"All right, J. D.," Tom ordered. "Pull up the coaster."

I pulled the coaster up the track while Tom climbed up to the roof. He brought a hammer and a sixteen-penny nail with him. He drove the nail through the shingles and sheathing.

"I'll hold the coaster," he said, "while you coil up the rope and wrap it around that nail so it won't slide off the roof."

I did as I was told. Then Tom told me to brace my feet and hold the coaster while he got into it. A moment later the chute-the-chute was ready for its first trial run. I was holding the coaster by the rear end.

"Now, J. D.," Tom said, "before you let go always make

74

sure you've removed the rope from the hook on the coaster. Let her rip!"

I let go of the coaster and down the track it went, lickety-split. It went so fast that when it hit the ground it traveled about twenty-five feet in the dirt before stopping. Right away Parley, Seth, and Danny wanted to ride.

"I guess you are entitled to one ride free for helping," Tom said.

He pulled the coaster back to the bottom of the track and hollered up at me to throw down the rope. He took the end with the loop on it and fastened it to the hook on the coaster.

"Pull her up!" he shouted.

Then both he and Parley came up to the roof. I was holding the coaster.

"Pull the rear wheels back over the brace and the coaster will hold itself," Tom said. "That will give you a chance to coil up the rope after each ride and unhook the coaster."

I did as he ordered.

"Now, J. D.," Tom said, "lift those rear wheels back on the track and hold the coaster with both hands while Parley gets into it."

A moment later the coaster was all set for its second trip. I let go and it went flying down the track and again traveled about twenty-five feet on the ground after leaving the track.

"Now, Parley," Tom shouted, "whoever rides the coaster must bring it back, set it on the track, and attach the rope to the hook so J. D. can pull the coaster back up."

Seth and Danny both took their free ride. Tom wouldn't let Frankie or me ride in the coaster until after Papa inspected it. He put the coaster in the barn so no kids could steal any free rides.

Papa didn't get a chance to inspect the track and coaster until after Sunday dinner, which we always ate at one o'clock. He tried to shake the track but it was too solid. He even grabbed hold of it and lifted himself off the ground to see if it would hold his weight. Then he inspected the coaster. He turned it over.

"You did a good job of securing the axle to the coaster," he told Tom. "Those front wheels will take quite a jolt coming off the chute-the-chute. Now let's have a demonstration."

I climbed up on the roof of the barn and tossed down the rope. Tom hooked the loop on the hook. I pulled the coaster to the top while Tom climbed up the ladder. A moment later Tom was seated in the coaster and ready to go.

"Let go now, J. D.," he said.

Down the track the coaster went, lickety-split, hitting the ground and going on about twenty-five feet. Tom pulled it back to the track.

"Well, Papa," he said. "I guess you've got to admit that the track and coaster are perfectly safe."

"Yes, they are," Papa said, "if you operate them properly. You must make sure that J. D. removes the rope from the hook before each ride. Otherwise the rope could become snagged, stop suddenly, and pitch whoever was riding in the coaster out of it."

"I'll make sure of it," Tom said, "on each and every ride."

A crowd of about twenty kids had arrived. Tom waited until Papa left and then made what he called a pitch.

"All right, fellows," he shouted, "line up for the ride of a lifetime on the chute-the-chute. Just a penny a ride in cash, no credit or promises. The thrill of a lifetime for only a penny."

The kids lined up. Tom stood at the foot of the ladder to collect a penny from each one. I wasn't worried about the chute-the-chute, but I began to worry about the ladder because there was a kid on every step of it waiting for his turn to ride. Seth Smith, who had already ridden on the coaster, was first in line. I pulled the coaster to the top and put the rear wheels over the brace to hold it while I coiled up the rope.

Tom yelled up at me, "Is the coaster unhooked?"

"Right," I shouted.

"Then take it off the brace and hold it with both hands for our first customer," Tom shouted.

I obeyed orders. Seth got into the coaster. I let go. When the coaster stopped on the ground, Seth pulled it back to the track and attached the loop of the rope to the hook. The chute-the-chute was open for business.

It only took about two minutes for each ride, which meant Tom was making thirty cents an hour. He kept his word to Papa, calling up each time to make sure I'd unhooked the rope, which seemed sort of silly to me. We had to quit at four o'clock so the fellows could go home and do their evening chores. Tom had collected eighty-four cents besides giving Frankie his ten free rides. That meant I'd pulled the coaster back up the track ninety-four times. No wonder there were blisters on my hands. I was doing all the work and Tom was making all the money. Thirty kids could ride in one hour. That meant I was only making three cents an hour.

I let Tom know how I felt when he paid me eight cents and told me the extra four rides would count on the next day.

"I do all the work and you make all the money," I said, showing him the blisters on my hands. "I should be a fifty-percent partner or at least a twenty-five-percent partner."

"Don't be silly," Tom said. "Out of the goodness of my heart I'm making you a ten-percent partner."

"Well, you had better make it a twenty-five-percent partner or I quit," I said, feeling positive that Tom would do it knowing I was doing all the work.

"You're being a fool," Tom said. "I'll be able to run the chute-the-chute for an hour and a half on school days and for several hours on weekends. I'll be taking in four or five dollars a week and your ten percent will be forty or fifty cents. But if you want to be a fool it's all right with me. I'll get somebody else to help me run the chute-the-chute."

Maybe it was because of the blisters on my hands, or maybe because I'd helped build the track, or maybe because I was doing all the work that I felt so stubborn.

"Twenty-five percent or I quit," I said.

"So you quit," Tom said, looking unconcerned. "And to show you my heart is in the right place I only owe you four-tenths of a cent but here is a penny."

That evening after supper Tom left the house. He returned in about an hour. I was still hurt that he wouldn't make me a twenty-five-percent partner, but the more I thought about it the more I began to regret that I'd quit. I guess that's what made me stay awake until he came up to bed.

"I've changed my mind," I said when Tom came into the bedroom. "I've decided not to quit."

"You're too late," Tom said. "I made a deal with Pete Kyle tonight to help me run the chute-the-chute. And you should have that little brain of yours examined. I offered you a chance to make four times as much money each week as you make doing your share of the chores."

Tom was right. It was hard work carrying in kindling wood and coal for the stoves. It was hard work milking the cow. It was hard work pitching hay into the manger for the livestock. All chores were hard work. It took Tom and Frankie and me at least one hour every morning before breakfast and one hour in the evening to do the chores. I was working fourteen hours a week for ten cents allowance. And I'd been fool enough not to be satisfied making three cents an hour working with Tom on the chute-the-chute. Boy, oh, boy, sometimes my little brain was so dumb it astounded me.

"Can't you call the deal off with Pete?" I asked. "After all, I am your own flesh and blood."

"Everybody knows that when I make a deal, I keep my word," Tom said. "Anyway, I'll feel safer with Pete up there helping me because he is older and bigger than you."

Boy, oh, boy, it was bad enough to lose the job without having Tom rub salt in my wounds. I had a heck of a time going to sleep that night because I kept myself awake by thinking of what a fool I'd been.

During the next couple of weeks I had to get in line and pay a penny just like everybody else to ride the chute-the-chute. No wonder Tom had customers lined up. It was like flying through the air. It was so fast that the wind whistled in my ears. I'd never had such a thrill in my life. I took more than twenty-five rides on the chute-the-chute, paying each time. I couldn't help being jealous of Pete, although I knew his family was poor and he needed the money. But I sure wasn't jealous when the accident happened.

Parley Benson was the passenger. Pete forgot to unhook

the rope from the coaster, and he was standing with one foot inside the coil of rope on the roof. His foot got tangled up with the rope when the coaster was about halfway down the track. Pete was pulled off the roof and Parley went flying out of the coaster head over heels. It was a wonder Parley didn't break his neck, but all he got were a few bruises. But Pete was lying on the ground with his right leg in a strange position.

"My leg!" Pete cried out and then fainted.

I ran to the house and got Mamma to phone Dr. LeRoy. When the doctor arrived he said Pete's leg was broken. He had Pete taken to our small county hospital where he set the leg and put it in a cast. Mamma had phoned Papa and Mr. and Mrs. Kyle. Papa went to the hospital with Pete's parents. When he returned he didn't say anything until after we had supper and were all sitting in the parlor.

"I told Mr. and Mrs. Kyle that I will pay all of the doctor and hospital bills," he said.

Tom looked up from a book he was reading. "Why should you pay anything?" he asked. "It was Pete's fault. He forgot to unhook the rope from the coaster."

"Mr. and Mrs. Kyle could sue me if they were that kind of people," Papa said. "But that isn't the reason why I'm going to pay the bills. In the first place it wasn't Pete's fault. It was your fault. I warned you about making certain the rope was unhooked. You didn't do it."

"I didn't think I had to with Pete," Tom said. "I figured he was old enough and smart enough that I didn't have to remind him like I did with J. D."

It only took a little brain to figure out that Tom was indirectly saying I was a dummy. I was astonished when Papa seemed to agree with him.

"That doesn't excuse your carelessness," Papa said. "When a person goes into any kind of business he automatically becomes responsible for the welfare and safety of his employees."

"But a thing like that wouldn't ever happen again," Tom protested.

"I am going to make sure it doesn't," Papa said. "You will tear down the chute-the-chute and destroy the coaster."

"But you said it was perfectly safe," Tom said. "It is the best money-maker my great brain ever invented."

"It isn't safe when you don't take every precaution to make certain an accident can't happen," Papa said. "And now for your punishment for letting this accident happen which you could have avoided by making certain the coaster was unhooked before each ride."

"Punishment?" Tom asked bug-eyed. "Having to tear down the chute-the-chute is more than enough punishment."

"It is only the beginning of your punishment," Papa said. "I know that you know to a penny how much you made with the chute-the-chute. You will turn all that money over to me to help pay the doctor and hospital bills. And you will report to Mrs. Kyle every day and do the chores Pete used to do before he broke his leg. You will not hire anybody to do them. I want you to do them yourself and continue to do them until Pete is able to do them himself."

"But that means I won't have time to do my share of chores at home," Tom protested. "I'll lose my allowance and get nothing for doing all of Pete's chores."

"Exactly," Papa said. "And this should teach you that going into any kind of business is more than just trying to make money."

Boy, oh, boy, what a catastrophe for The Great Brain.

82

Giving up the twelve dollars and forty cents he had made with the chute-the-chute would break his money-loving heart into a thousand pieces. Doing Pete's chores would make him wish he'd never seen a chute-the-chute.

"Boy," I said to Tom, "am I glad you didn't make me a twenty-five-percent partner."

"I was coming to you," Papa said. "You helped to build the chute-the-chute and were a partner for one day. You will hand over to me the eight cents commission you were paid. And, because if you hadn't gotten greedy and wanted twenty-five percent instead of ten percent this accident would not have happened, your punishment will be no allowance for a month."

I'm telling you, there are times when a fellow just can't win, especially where parents are concerned. I knew if Mr. and Mrs. Kyle had sued Papa that Judge Potter wouldn't have blamed me for the accident. The judge would have to go by what is written in the law books. But, you take a father, he just makes up his own laws as he goes along, and boy, oh, boy, there ought to be a law against that.

CHAPTER SIX

Tom Becomes an Indian Blood Brother

WE HAD OUR FIRST INDIAN TROUBLE soon after Papa put Tom out of the chute-the-chute business. During the 1890s the last of the Indians in southwestern Utah were placed on reservations. Several tribes were confined to the Shivwits-Shebit Reservation near Santa Clara, Utah. Other Indians were placed on two small reservations including the Pa-Roos-Its band of Paiute Indians who were placed on a reservation about ten miles from Adenville.

Before being placed on the reservation Chief Tav-Whad-Im, which translated into English means Rising Sun, and his band of Pa-Roos-Its never made any trouble for the citizens of Adenville. This was due to the fact that the Mormons had always treated the Indians very well. It was part of their religion. They believed the American Indians were Lamanites descended from the white tribe of Joseph, who were led by the Prophet Lehi from Jerusalem to the western hemisphere in 600 B.C. They treated the Indians as brothers.

The Paiutes had been driven from their good hunting and fishing grounds by white men before being put on the reservation. The Mormons tried to make up for this by giving the Chief and his band flour, potatoes, turnips, corn, and other food from the church storehouse. And the Gentile ranchers contributed sheep, hogs, and cattle. The people in town collected old clothing and enough money to buy medicine. The Paiutes came into Adenville to sell beaded buckskin gloves, moccasins, jackets, furs, roasted pine nuts, and other things. Papa had invited Chief Rising Sun to our house for Sunday dinner several times.

When the United States government put the Chief and his band on the Pa-Roos-Its reservation all of this stopped. James Fredericks, the Indian agent, under orders from the State Superintendent of Indian Affairs, stated that the government would furnish the Paiutes with all the food, supplies, clothing, and medicine they needed, but the Paiutes were not allowed to leave the reservation. A Mission School was established on the reservation to teach the Paiutes how to speak, read, and write in English.

Papa and Bishop Aden were both worried when the Indians were first placed on the reservation. They knew some Indian agents were dishonest and cheated the Indians. They waited two months and then went to see Chief Rising Sun, making sure Mr. Fredericks wasn't with them when they entered the Chief's tepee. They asked the Chief how the Indian agent was treating him and his band.

"Mr. Fredericks," Chief Rising Sun told them, "wears an Indian moccasin on his left foot and a white man's shoe on his right foot and is our *tubicin*."

This was the Chief's way of saying Mr. Fredericks was honest and fair in his dealings with the Indians and they considered him their friend. *Tubicin* in their language meant friend.

We had no Indian trouble until Mr. Fredericks died from a heart attack several years later. A new Indian agent named Henry Parker took his place. Mr. Parker was much tougher with the Indians. He was what Papa called "a stickler for rules and regulations." He had been Indian agent for about four months when a Paiute whose English name was Hail Storm came to our back door one night. Mamma cooked him some ham and eggs, which he wolfed down as if he were half-starved. Then Papa took him into the parlor to talk.

"I know," Papa said, "that you didn't get Mr. Parker's permission to leave the reservation because you came here at night. I also know you came to me because I am a friend of Chief Rising Sun. Why are you here?"

"Chief Tav-Whad-Im sent me," Hail Storm said. "He wants to see you and Bishop Aden and Sheriff Baker. I go now."

Papa left the next morning with Bishop Aden in the Bishop's buggy and Sheriff Baker riding his horse. Of course, he wouldn't let Tom and me go with them, but he promised to tell us all about it later.

A building that was the combination office, trading post, and home of Henry Parker was in the center of the reservation. In the Indian village surrounding it men, women, and children sat in front of their tepees staring at the three men as they passed.

"They look listless to me," Papa said.

"They look hungry to me," Bishop Aden said. "Look, even the children are not running around and playing. There is definitely something wrong here."

Mr. Parker, who was sitting on the porch of the building, saw them coming and walked down the steps to meet them. He was a tall, gaunt man with a sallow complexion and a black moustache. He already knew Papa, Bishop Aden, and Sheriff Baker.

"Hello, gentlemen," he said. "To what do I owe this unexpected visit?"

Sheriff Baker dismounted. "We want to talk to Chief Rising Sun in private," he said.

"According to the book of rules and regulations," Mr. Parker said, "I could refuse to let you do it. Nobody is allowed on an Indian reservation unless they are a United States Marshal or work for the Bureau of Indian Affairs. However, since I know all of you personally, I believe I can make an exception. You will find Chief Rising Sun in his tepee. I believe I know why you are here. But listen to his story first and then we will talk."

Papa, Bishop Aden, and Sheriff Baker entered the tepee of the Chief. After greeting them Chief Rising Sun asked them to sit down on the buffalo robe in his tepee.

Bishop Aden spoke first. "You sent for us," he said. "We are your friends. Why did you want to see us?"

"When Mr. Fredericks was Indian agent," Chief Rising Sun said, "there was enough food, medicine, clothing, and supplies for my people. Two months ago Mr. Parker told me the government has cut rations for all Indian reservations by twenty-five percent. There are no longer enough supplies for my people. I am afraid many of my young braves will leave the reservation and become renegades."

Papa was surprised. "I don't remember reading anything in the *New York World* weekly mail-edition about this," he said.

Bishop Aden shrugged. "Perhaps they didn't think it important enough to print," he said. "Since putting the Indians on reservations many white people just want to forget they ever existed."

Sheriff Baker was skeptical. "How do we know Mr. Parker is telling the truth?" he asked. "Some of the Indian agents the government sends are out-and-out thieves."

"That we will find out," Bishop Aden said. "Meanwhile, Chief Rising Sun, the Church of Jesus Christ of Latter-day Saints will see that you have enough food to make up for the twenty-five-percent cut. And I'm sure the Gentiles will see that you get steers, hogs, and sheep to slaughter for meat. And we will all see that you have clothing and medicine."

"Thank you, *tubicin,*" Chief Rising Sun said.

They bade goodbye to the Chief. Mr. Parker was waiting for them.

"I suppose," he said, "Chief Rising Sun has told you about the government cutting reservation allotments by twenty-five percent."

Bishop Aden nodded. "Yes," he said, "and we have promised to make up that twenty-five percent."

"That is mighty generous of you," Mr. Parker said. "I'm sure these poor devils will appreciate it as much as I do."

Sheriff Baker hitched his thumbs in his gun belt. "No offense, Mr. Parker," he said, "but before we leave we would like to see proof that the rations have been cut."

"I suppose I should be offended," Mr. Parker said, "but I'm not. I found it hard to believe when I was notified. Come into my office, gentlemen, and I'll show you proof."

In the office Mr. Parker opened two drawers in a file cabinet and removed two folders. He opened them on his desk and pointed at one of them.

"Here are copies of requisitions and bills of lading while Mr. Fredericks was Indian agent and for two months while I was the agent," he said.

Then he opened the other folder. "Here are requisitions and bills of lading for the past two months," he said. "If you compare them you will find every item from beans to tobacco has been cut twenty-five percent. All food, clothing, medicine, and supplies for all three reservations in southwestern Utah are shipped to the Shivwits-Shebit reservation in Santa Clara because it is so much larger. From their warehouse the monthly allotments of rations are shipped here and to the other reservation. I was notified two months ago of the cut in rations by the Supply Master at the Shivwits-Shebit reservation."

Papa, Bishop Aden, and Sheriff Baker examined the requisitions and bills of lading. They could readily see the allotments for the Pa-Roos-Its reservation had been cut twenty-five percent during the past two months.

Bishop Aden shook his head. "The government is barely giving the Indians enough food to survive," he said.

"It just so happens," Mr. Parker said, "that our monthly rations are arriving by wagon train the day after tomorrow.

To satisfy Chief Rising Sun, I would appreciate it if you three gentlemen were on hand to check the supplies against the requisitions and bills of lading. I get the feeling that Chief Rising Sun thinks I'm lying to him."

The following day the Mormons sent a wagonload of food to the reservation from their church storehouse. Ranchers contributed sheep, hogs, and beef. People in Adenville collected old clothing and money for medicine to send.

Papa admitted he had his doubts until he, Bishop Aden, and Sheriff Baker went to the reservation when the freight wagons arrived with the monthly allotment. They checked the bills of lading against every item. Everything was in order. There was just seventy-five percent as much as the reservation used to receive.

That evening after supper Papa sat smoking his after-dinner cigar and staring into space. Mamma looked up from her sewing.

"What's bothering you?" she asked.

"It's a shame," Papa said, "the way the Indians are treated. First we broke one treaty after another with them. Then we drove them from their hunting and fishing grounds into barren land. Then we herded them onto reservations and promised to feed and clothe them and take care of them. Then some muddle-headed Congressmen who think Indians are being treated too well cut the appropriations for the Bureau of Indian Affairs by twenty-five percent. I've half a mind to write a blistering editorial about it and mail a copy to every Senator and every member of the House of Representatives."

Mamma shook her head. "I doubt if they would pay any

attention to one little newspaper from a small town," she said.

"You're right, of course," Papa said. "Well, at least, thanks to Bishop Aden and the Mormons and the Gentiles in this county, the Indians on the Pa-Roos-Its reservation will have plenty to eat and enough clothing, supplies, and medicine. We will more than make up for that twenty-five percent cut."

Tom, who had been listening, got up from his chair and stood with one elbow on the mantelpiece.

"I just can't believe the President of the United States and the Congress could be so mean," he said. "Are you sure Mr. Parker is an honest Indian agent?"

"I had my doubts," Papa said, "until we checked the monthly shipment from the Shivwits-Shebit reservation. Mr. Parker is an honest Indian agent. The blame lies with Congress and President McKinley for cutting the appropriations."

The next day was Saturday. Frankie and I finished the morning chores and Eddie Huddle came over to play with Frankie. I sat on the back porch steps waiting for Tom, who was doing Pete Kyle's chores. Tom didn't get home until eleven o'clock.

"Boy, oh, boy," I said, "poor old Pete must have a lot of chores to do. Frankie and I were finished two hours ago."

Tom sat down beside me. "Mrs. Kyle makes Pete do more than just chores," he said. "She made me help her wash the parlor and dining-room windows. This is the worst punishment Papa ever gave me."

Tom just sat there staring straight ahead. I thought he was thinking about having to do Pete's chores for the next

91

few weeks. But I was wrong.

"I can't get those poor Indians out of my mind," he finally said. "I lay awake for a long time last night thinking about them."

"Well," I said, "at least the Indians on our reservation are going to be taken care of."

"But what about all the other Indians on reservations all over the country?" Tom asked. Then he stood up. "I am going to write a letter to the President of the United States denouncing him and Congress."

"Can I watch?" I asked, because I'd never seen anybody write a letter to the President.

"Get me a writing tablet, an envelope, and a pencil," Tom said.

I went into the house and got the writing materials. Then I followed Tom to the barn and up the rope ladder to his loft. He opened the tablet and laid it on a box. He sat down cross-legged. He wet the lead in the pencil with his tongue and then he began to write. But he only wrote a few words before he tore the page from the tablet and crumpled it up.

"What did you say?" I asked. "What did you say?"

"It isn't every day in the year a fellow writes to the President of the United States," Tom said. "I want to tell him off but I've got to be sort of polite about it."

Tom wrote and destroyed six more pages before he finally completed the letter. He read it several times and then handed it to me.

"See what you think, J. D.," he said.

The letter read:

Dear President McKinley:

I am only twelve years old and not old enough to vote. But I am a citizen of the United States and that entitles me to write a letter to the President. Just what kind of a man are you anyway? It was bad enough for Presidents to break treaties with the Indians and herd them like cattle onto reservations. But at least the Indians got enough to eat until you and Congress cut the appropriations for the Bureau of Indian Affairs, and now the poor Indians only get seventy-five percent as much food, clothing, supplies, and medicine as they used to get. How would you like it if somebody took away twenty-five percent of your food? I'll bet you wouldn't like it at all. So what makes you think the Indians will like it? My father voted for you but I'll bet he'll never vote for a man like you again. You and Congress make me sick.

Yours truly,

Tom D. Fitzgerald

"Boy, oh, boy," I said when I finished reading the letter, "you had better not mail this unless you want to go to prison. You can't insult the President like this and get away with it."

"They can't put you in prison for telling the truth," Tom said.

I went with him to the post office. I watched him buy a stamp and put it on the envelope. I made one last effort to stop him.

"They'll send the Secret Service to arrest you for lambasting the President that way," I said. "Please don't mail the letter."

"Let them," Tom said, and then walked over and

93

dropped the letter in the mailbox.

Tom went to the post office every day, but ten days passed before he finally received a letter in a White House envelope in our mailbox. Mr. Olsen the postmaster stopped us.

"Didn't know you had friends in the White House, Tom," he said.

"This is a letter from the President of the United States," Tom said.

"I'd have to see that to believe it," Mr. Olsen said.

"Then I'll show you," Tom said. But he sure looked disappointed when he saw the letter.

"It's from his secretary," he said.

Tom waited until we got outside the post office to read the letter which read:

Dear Master Tom D. Fitzgerald:

The President has asked me to answer your letter to let you know that all Indians on all reservations are receiving the same allotment of food, clothing, supplies, and medicine that they have always received. If you know of any Indians who aren't receiving their just share, have your father get in touch with the State Superintendent of Indian Affairs in Salt Lake City and report it.

Yours truly,
Peter Evans
Secretary to the President

I handed the letter back to Tom.

"This," he said holding up the letter, "proves that Henry Parker is a crook and is cheating the Paiutes on the reservation."

94

"Are you going to do what the letter says and have Papa report him?" I asked.

"No," Tom said. "I'm going to show the letter to Sheriff Baker and have him arrest that crook Henry Parker."

Uncle Mark and Sheriff Baker were sitting at their desks when we entered the combination marshal and sheriff's office. Tom let both of them read the letter after telling them he had written to the President.

"That proves Henry Parker is a crook," he said.

Sheriff Baker shook his head. "No, it doesn't, Tom," he said. "It only proves that somebody at the Shivwits-Shebit reservation is cheating the Pa-Roos-Its band."

Uncle Mark nodded. "What they must be doing," he said, "is making out two requisitions and two bills of lading. They send the fake one with the wagons that bring the supplies. They keep the real one and send copies to the State Superintendent of Indian Affairs."

"Right," Sheriff Baker said. "I think our best bet is to send a telegram to the State Superintendent of Indian Affairs in Salt Lake City and have him send us a United States Marshal and somebody from his office."

A United States Marshal named Thomas and a man named Anderson from the office of the State Superintendent of Indian Affairs arrived the next morning on the eleven o'clock train. Tom and I were in school but Uncle Mark told us everything later. He showed the two men the letter from the Secretary to the President. Mr. Anderson said there had been no cut in the allotment for the Shivwits-Shebit reservation or the two smaller reservations.

They went to the Pa-Roos-Its reservation. Henry Parker

knew the game was up. He confessed and offered to turn state's evidence against Benjamin Wagner, the Supply Master at the Shivwits-Shebit reservation. It was a neat scheme Wagner had worked out with Henry Parker and an Indian agent named Halpern on the other reservation. Wagner sold the surplus twenty-five percent of the rations to his brother, who ran a trading post. He kept fifty percent of the money and gave twenty-five percent to Parker and twenty-five percent to Halpern. Wagner confessed when confronted by Parker and Halpern, both of whom offered to turn state's evidence. The three men were tried in the Federal Court in Salt Lake City and all were given prison terms.

Then one Saturday during lunch Papa told Tom and me to hitch up our team to our buggy.

"We are going to the reservation," he said. "Chief Rising Sun wants to see you, T. D."

Papa let Frankie and me go along. The new Indian agent, a man named Haley, met us at the reservation. Papa told Frankie and me to stay with Mr. Haley. He and Tom walked to the tepee of Chief Rising Sun. The Chief and his council were sitting in a circle in front of his tepee. Papa and Tom sat down. The Chief lit a pipe. He took a few puffs and then passed it around. Everybody except Tom took a few puffs. Then the Chief began to chant in the Uto-Aztecan language of the tribe. Mr. Haley, Frankie, and I were standing near enough to hear. Mr. Haley knew the language. He said the Chief was singing praises to Tom for getting rid of Henry Parker and saving the tribe. Then the Chief stood up. He handed the pipe to a squaw and motioned for Tom to stand beside him. He held out his left wrist. He motioned for

Tom to hold out his right wrist. Then a member of the council cut each wrist just enough to make it bleed. The Chief grasped Tom's bleeding wrist and held it against his own. He spoke first in the Uto-Aztecan language and then in English:

"Hail to our blood brother! Hail to The Boy Who Wrote The Great White Father A Letter And Saved The Pa-Roos-Its Band."

The Chief let go of Tom's wrist. Two squaws immediately bandaged Tom's and the Chief's wrists. Then the council stood up. They raised their right arms and spoke in the Uto-Aztecan language. Mr. Haley said they were saying, "Hail to our blood brother. Hail to The Boy Who Wrote The Great White Father A Letter And Saved The Pa-Roos-Its Band." Then some of the tribe began beating on tom-toms and the young braves began to dance. They began to chant, "Hail to our blood brother," some in English and some in their own language. When the dance ended the Chief and his council and Papa and Tom sat down. The Chief motioned for Mr. Haley, Frankie, and me to join them.

"We are going to have an Indian feast," Mr. Haley said.

All I can say is that when Indians decide to have a feast they aren't fooling. Squaws brought wooden bowls with boiled mutton, roast pig, jackrabbit stew, Indian corn bread, and so many other things I can't remember all of them. The feast lasted two hours. I was so full I was bursting, but Papa said if I didn't eat at least a bite of everything it would be an insult to the Chief.

And that is how I got the worst bellyache of my life, and how Tom became a blood brother of the Pa-Roos-Its band of

Paiutes, with the strange and long name of The Boy Who Wrote The Great White Father A Letter And Saved The Pa-Roos-Its Band.

CHAPTER SEVEN

Herbie the Poet

TOM WAS SO BUSY doing all of Pete Kyle's chores and helping Papa with printing jobs that he didn't have time to pull any swindles for a while. It was just a few days after Pete was well enough to do his own chores that Papa told us during supper a new family named Sties had arrived in town. Mr. Sties was going to take the place of Mr. Colopy, who had died suddenly of a heart attack. Mr. Colopy had been the bookkeeper at the bank. Mrs. Colopy had decided to sell their home and go back East to live with relatives. The Sties family bought the house.

We were having fish for supper because it was Friday. And boy, oh, boy, when Mamma cooked codfish you could

100

smell it all over town. I admit it tasted all right, but for my money Mamma should have given everybody at the table a clothespin to put on their nose. Tom liked all kinds of fish because he said fish was good for the brain. He was putting away his second helping of codfish when Papa finished.

"Do they have any kids?" Tom asked.

"One son," Papa answered.

Mamma said, "I shall call on Mrs. Sties as soon as she has put up her lace curtains."

Small-town etiquette was funny in those days. A new family moved into town but nobody would call on them until they saw the lace curtains hanging in the parlor. That meant everything was unpacked and in its proper place. Then the ladies would call and leave a calling card which was like an invitation for the new family to call on them.

The next day was Saturday. After morning chores I went with Tom and Frankie to Smith's vacant lot. There were about twenty of us playing different games when we all stopped to stare at the new kid in town coming toward us. He was the fattest boy I'd ever seen. He looked to be about ten or eleven years old and he was so fat that he made Tubby Ralston look skinny. He had such a fat round face that you couldn't tell where his jaw ended and his chin began. He walked up and spoke to us:

"Hello fellows, my name is Herbie Sties.

Ask me no questions and I'll tell you no lies."

We all stared at him bug-eyed. Tom finally said what was on all our minds.

"How can we find out where you came from if we don't ask you any questions?" he asked.

Again Herbie spoke:

"We lived in Salt Lake City
And would be living there still
If my father hadn't come home one day and said
We're off, we're off to Adenville."

Parley pushed his coonskin cap to the back of his head.
"This kid is some kind of a freak," he said.

Herbie looked at him and said:
"Maybe you're too dumb to know it
But I'm no freak. I'm Herbie the poet."

Herbie was younger and smaller than Parley. But Parley
became so angry he grabbed Herbie and began shaking the
fat boy.

"Don't you dare call me dumb, you fat freak," he said.

Did that scare Herbie? Heck no. He looked Parley right
straight in the eyes.

"I'm not afraid to fight you
As sure as my name is Herbie Sties,
Although I know if I do fight you
I'll end up with two black eyes."

Tom put a hand on Parley's shoulder. "Let him go," he
said. Then he looked at Herbie. "Do you always talk like
that?"

Herbie nodded.

"I always make up rhymes except in school
Where as you know it's against the rule."

"But why do you make up rhymes instead of talking like
other kids?" Tom asked.

Herbie dropped his head as if ashamed.

"I can't play football or baseball,
I'm too fat to play any game at all.
I can't even play run-sheep-run
Because I'm too fat to catch anyone.

So instead of playing I make up a rhyme
To help me pass away the time."

Tom patted the fat boy on the shoulder. "Forget the poetry for a while," he said. "Are your mother and father fat like you?"

"Nope," Herbie said. "Just me."

"Then it isn't inherited," Tom said. "You must be fat because you are a greedy gut. Have you ever tried to take off weight by not eating candy, ice cream, desserts, and things like that?"

"My father said he'd give me ten cents a pound for every pound I lost," Herbie said. "I tried it once and lost one pound. But I spent the ten cents on candy. It's no use. I was just born to be fat and that is why I'm a poet."

Tom got that old conniving look on his face. "Ten cents a pound," he said. "Come over to my place. I want to talk to you."

Frankie and I followed Tom and Herbie to our barn. They sat down on a bale of hay.

"Now, Herbie," Tom said, "would your father still give you ten cents for each pound of fat you lose?"

"Sure," Herbie said. "He is always trying to get me to lose some weight."

"Wouldn't you like to lose enough weight so you could play and have fun like other kids?" Tom asked.

Herbie got a dreamy look in his eyes.

"There isn't anything that I wouldn't do
To be able to play and have fun like you."

"Good," Tom said. "My great brain will help you lose weight so you can play and have fun just like other kids."

Herbie's eyes became wide. "Your great brain?" he asked.

103

"You're new in town," Tom said, "and don't know about my great brain. There isn't anything I can't do with my great brain. Ask any kid in town. But I don't use my great brain for nothing. I'll make you a business proposition. You give me the ten cents a pound that your father will give you and I'll have you weighing no more than any other kid your age in town."

"How?" Herbie asked.

"With my own special exercises for taking off weight," Tom said. "And you'll have to promise to go on a diet and not eat any more candy or other sweets."

Herbie began to shake his head with a sad expression on his face.

"No more candy, no more cakes,
No more pies my mother bakes.
I'm sorry but I cannot tell a lie—
Without any sweets I know I'll die."

Tom lifted up his shoulders with a sort of "who cares" look on his face.

"If you'd rather be a tub of fat and not have any fun like other kids, that is up to you," he said. "You can just go on being a poet and a greedy gut."

"I didn't say I wouldn't," Herbie said. "I'll try."

Tom got up from the bale of hay. "Just to keep the record straight," he said very businesslike, "we will go to Dr. LeRoy's office and weigh you naked. And every Saturday we'll do the same thing to see how much weight you lost during the week. You'll collect ten cents for each pound you lose from your father and give it to me. Is it a deal?"

Herbie nodded and they shook hands to seal the bargain.

I didn't think Dr. LeRoy would like the idea of a non-paying patient using his scales and his office. But after Tom explained he was going to help Herbie lose weight, Dr. LeRoy let him weigh Herbie naked on the scales. Herbie weighed ninety-six pounds. Dr. LeRoy then measured Herbie's height and asked Herbie's age. Herbie said he was ten years old.

"For a boy your age and height," Dr. LeRoy said, "you should only weigh about seventy pounds. You really should go on a diet and do exercises to help you reduce. Being overweight can effect your heart and circulatory system and shorten your life."

Tom really poured it on Herbie when we left the doctor's office. "You heard what Dr. LeRoy said. If you don't get rid of about twenty-six pounds of that blubber you will be dead in a few years. Meet me in our barn after lunch and my great brain will save you from an early grave."

We had about half an hour before lunch when we got home. Tom got a book he'd sent away for one time entitled *The Home Reference Library*. It had everything in it from how to draw up a will to how to make homemade cough syrup. Tom opened the book to where it described exercises for taking off weight and studied them.

After lunch Eddie Huddle came over to play with Frankie. I went to the barn with Tom. Herbie arrived a few minutes later.

"All right, Herbie," Tom said. "Let's get started. We are going to do one hour of exercises after school on school days and two hours of exercises on Saturdays."

Tom made Herbie lie flat on his back on the floor of the barn. He told Herbie to lift up his legs and touch his stomach with his knees ten times. Herbie was so fat he couldn't even do it once.

"We'll try another one," Tom said as he grabbed Herbie's ankles and lifted up the fat boy's legs. "Now just lie on your back and pump your legs as if you are riding a bicycle."

He made Herbie do that until the fat boy was exhausted. He let Herbie rest for a couple of minutes. Then he told Herbie to stand up and bend over and touch his toes ten times. Herbie could only reach to his kneecaps. Tom made him bend over and touch his knees ten times. Herbie was puffing and sweating when he finished. Tom let him rest a couple of minutes and then continued with other weight-reducing exercises until Herbie just up and quit.

"I'm pooped," Herbie said, puffing hard as sweat poured off him.

Tom sat down on a bale of hay. "Take a little rest and then we'll run around the block a few times," he said.

For my money I didn't think Herbie could run around the block more than one time, and I was right. He ran around once with Tom and me and then sat down in the alley and refused to move.

"No more," Herbie cried, painfully gasping for breath.

"All right," Tom said. "We'll call it quits for today and we'll take tomorrow off because it is Sunday. But you be here Monday right after school lets out."

Herbie had sweat running down his fat cheeks and was still puffing hard. "Nope," he said. "I quit."

"You quit on me," Tom said, "and I'll get every kid in town to call you Fatso. And I'll get them to make so much fun of you for being fat that you'll wish you were dead."

Herbie got to his feet and began to cry. Then he ran down the alley. Tom watched until Herbie turned the corner. He had a grin on his freckled face.

"If he runs all the way home," Tom said, "that should take a few ounces off him."

"What good will that do?" I asked. "He said that he quit."

"He'll be back," Tom said confidently, "after he thinks it over."

The Great Brain was right. We were doing our evening chores when Herbie came down the alley. He didn't say anything as he handed Tom a piece of paper. Then he went back up the alley. Tom read what was on the paper and began laughing as he handed it to me.

"What did I tell you?" Tom said.

Herbie had written a poem which read:

To Tom Fitzgerald and his Great Brain
I thought I never wanted to see you again
But there is one thing I know
I don't want to be called Fatso
So I guess it is my fate
To let you help me take off weight.

Every afternoon after school during the following week Tom had Herbie doing exercises and running around the block until the fat boy was exhausted. Saturday morning I went with Tom and Herbie to Dr. LeRoy's office. And I'll be an elephant with two trunks if Herbie didn't weigh a pound more than he had the week before. Tom was completely mystified at first. We left Herbie and went home for lunch. After eating we sat on the back porch steps.

"You know, J. D.," Tom said, "there is something mighty fishy about Herbie gaining weight after all those exercises. When we finish the exercises this afternoon we'll follow him. I know he is cheating and not keeping his promise to cut out the candy and sweets."

Tom put Herbie through two hours of exercises that afternoon and made him run around the block four times. Then we followed Herbie without him knowing it. Herbie went straight to the drugstore. He was in there for a little while. Then he came out and went to the Z. C. M. I. store while Tom and I hid behind trees so he wouldn't see us. He came out of the store with a bag filled with something. We followed him and saw him go around in back of the Community Church. When we peeked around the corner Herbie was eating candy from the bag. Tom and I ran all the way back to the drugstore. Sammy Leeds was behind the soda fountain.

"You know Herbie Sties who just left here?" Tom asked.

"I should," Sammy said. "He is our best customer. Every day this week he has been coming here and eating a chocolate nut sundae."

Then Tom and I ran to the Z. C. M. I. store. Mr. Harmon was alone in the store.

"The fat boy who just left here," Tom said. "Has he been buying much candy from you, Mr. Harmon?"

"You mean Herbie Sties," Mr. Harmon said. "That is the candiest-eating boy I've ever seen. He has been stopping here every day this week and buying ten cents worth of candy."

"Thank you," Tom said.

Then Tom and I ran back to the Community Church. Herbie was just plopping a gumdrop into his mouth as we came upon him. He wadded up the empty bag and threw it away. He had eaten the whole ten cents worth of candy while we were gone. He looked like a kid caught with his hand in the cookie jar.

"Ah ha!" Tom said. "I caught you. No wonder you put on weight this week, eating chocolate nut sundaes at the drugstore and candy every day. And I'll bet you've been eating double desserts at home."

"I couldn't help it," Herbie pleaded. "All those exercises and running around the block made me so hungry I felt as if I was starving to death."

"I'm going to cure you of being a greedy gut or my name isn't T. D. Fitzgerald," Tom said. "Come with me."

We went to our barn. Tom climbed up to his loft and returned with an old Bible.

"Put your left hand on the Bible and raise your right hand," Tom ordered.

Herbie did as he was told.

"Now repeat after me," Tom said. "I, Herbie Sties, do solemnly swear on the Holy Bible to stop eating ice cream and candy and more than one dessert a day."

Herbie repeated the words.

Tom continued: "And if I break my sacred vow, my soul will belong to the Devil and I'll burn in everlasting Hell, so help me God."

Herbie turned a little pale but repeated the words.

"Now, Herbie," Tom said, "Sammy Leeds will let me know if you buy any more ice cream at the drugstore. And Mr. Harmon will let me know if you buy any more candy at the Z. C. M. I. store. And God and the Devil will know if you eat more than one dessert a day at home. And if you break your sacred oath your soul will belong to Satan and you will burn in everlasting Hell."

During the week that followed Tom checked every day with Sammy Leeds and Mr. Harmon. Herbie didn't buy any ice cream or candy. Tom increased the exercises and now had Herbie running around the block five times. He began

109

rubbing the palms of his hands together on Saturday morning as we sat on the back porch steps waiting for Herbie.

"I'll bet I took at least five pounds off of Herbie this week," he said. "And at ten cents a pound that comes to fifty cents."

"Herbie sure as heck doesn't look any thinner to me," I said.

"He has to be," Tom said confidently. "He might have lost more than five pounds."

Herbie arrived a few minutes later. We all went to Dr. LeRoy's office. And I'll be a frog that can't swim if Herbie had lost even one pound. Tom was sure down in the dumps when we left the doctor's office. But he didn't give up. He told Herbie to be in our barn that afternoon for exercises. When we got home Tom went up to his loft to put his great brain to work on why Herbie hadn't lost any weight. When he came down for lunch he told me his great brain had figured it out but he wouldn't tell me any more.

That afternoon Tom made Herbie exercise for two hours and run around the block six times. He waited until Herbie left and then turned to me.

"We are going to follow him," Tom said, "but don't let him see you."

We followed Herbie down Main Street ducking behind trees until we arrived at Smith's vacant lot. We peeked around trees from the street. Herbie called Danny Forester to one side. It looked as if he was giving Danny something. Then both of them began walking down Main Street. They parted at the Community Church. Herbie went around to the back and Danny continued on to the Z. C. M. I. store.

"My great brain was right," Tom said. "Herbie has got Danny buying candy for him."

110

Tom was only half right. When Danny met Herbie in back of the Community Church he had a big bag. Tom and I peeked around the corner of the church. Danny gave Herbie the bag. First Herbie took out two candy bars and gave one to Danny. They finished eating the candy bars and then Danny left to go back to Smith's vacant lot. Then Herbie took out a box of animal crackers and ate them. He followed this by eating some gumdrops and peppermint sticks. Then he took out a box of ginger snaps and ate them. Then he ate more candy.

"What a greedy gut," Tom whispered with disgust.

"Are you going to denounce him on the spot?" I asked.

"It wouldn't do any good," Tom said. "Let's go. I've got to put my great brain to work on this."

As we walked home I couldn't help asking a question. "Is Herbie's father rich?"

"I don't think so," Tom said. "He is just a bookkeeper at the bank."

"Then where is Herbie getting all the money he is spending?" I asked.

"When the Sties lived in Salt Lake City," Tom said, "Herbie had an allowance of fifty cents a week like a lot of kids in a big city. Mr. Sties is probably still giving him fifty cents a week not knowing kids in a small town only get an allowance of about ten cents a week."

"What are you going to do?" I asked. "Herbie took an oath on the Bible. You don't think that maybe he is a fellow who doesn't believe in God."

"Of course not," Tom said. "Herbie is such a greedy gut that his stomach convinced him the oath was just kid stuff, which it was. And I'll bet he is having double helpings of dessert at home."

111

"What do you mean?" I asked. "About the oath being kid stuff?"

"The only people who can administer an oath on the Bible are priests, ministers, judges, clerks of the court, and people like that," Tom explained. "But my great brain will figure out a way to convince Herbie the oath he took was a sacred vow."

When we got home Tom went up to his loft in the barn to put his great brain to work. He was smiling when he came down after about half an hour.

"My great brain did it," he said grinning. "If Satan sends one of his devils to claim Herbie's soul, that will convince Herbie it was a sacred vow."

"Nothing to it," I said, and couldn't help being a little sarcastic. "Just telephone Satan and tell him to send one of his devils to claim Herbie's soul."

"Don't be silly," Tom said. "You are going to be the devil. Come with me."

I followed Tom into our house and up to the attic. Mamma was a saver. She never threw anything away. With four boys someone could always wear hand-me-downs. Tom found the box in the attic where Mamma stored our Halloween costumes so they could be used again. He dug into the box until he found a red devil costume he had worn two years before.

"It will just fit you now," he said. "Tomorrow night Herbie Sties is going to get a visit from a devil."

The next morning after services at the Community Church Tom and I walked a couple of blocks with Herbie.

"Just wanted you to know," Tom said to Herbie, "that I haven't given up making you lose weight. Same time tomorrow after school in our barn. I know you haven't broken your sacred vow about eating ice cream or candy or Sammy Leeds and Mr. Harmon would have told me. And I know you are only eating one dessert a day at home or Satan would have sent one of his devils to claim your soul. I guess we will just have to increase the exercises."

That night Tom went upstairs with Frankie and me at eight o'clock. He told Papa and Mamma that he felt tired and was going to bed early. We had the devil's costume hidden in our bedroom clothes closet. I took off my clothes except for my underwear and shoes and put on the costume. It was a red suit with a tail and a combination headpiece and mask which had two horns in front and a face that looked like Satan's.

Frankie's eyes grew wide as he stared at me. "I know it is you, John," he said, "but you scare me."

Tom smiled. "Let's hope it scares the be-jabbers out of Herbie Sties," he said. "You go to bed, Frankie."

Tom removed the screen from our bedroom window. We climbed down the elm tree to the ground. Our two dogs came running to greet us. We locked them in the barn so they couldn't follow us. Then we sneaked down alleys and side streets until we were in back of Herbie's home. It was a one-storey house with two bedrooms.

"The back bedroom is Herbie's," Tom whispered. "I found out his parents let him stay up until eight-thirty. We'll get under the window. When he comes into the bedroom I'll boost you up. Put your face close to the windowpane so he gets a good look at you. And then motion with your finger as if you're calling him. Then touch me on the shoulder and I'll let you down. Let's go."

We were all set under the bedroom window when the

light was turned on. Tom boosted me up and held me. I could see Herbie sitting in a chair taking off his shoes. He didn't see me because his head was bent down. I knocked on the windowpane. Herbie lifted his head and stared at me with a look of terror on his face. He stood up and I could see his whole body was trembling as if it was made of jelly. His mouth opened and shut but no sound came out. I motioned with my finger as if I were calling him. His eyeballs began to roll around in their sockets and then he fell face forward on the floor. I touched Tom on the shoulder. He let me down.

"He fainted," I whispered.

"Good," Tom said. "That proves he's scared and really believes Satan sent a devil for his soul."

Tom erased our footprints with a gunnysack as we left the yard. We made it back home without being seen. We let the dogs out of the barn and then climbed up the elm tree to our bedroom. Tom sat down on his bed.

"If that doesn't cure Herbie of being a greedy gut," he said, "I don't know what will."

I removed the headpiece. "I still can't figure out how scaring Herbie is going to help," I said, keeping my voice low because Frankie was sleeping. "He'll figure he has nothing to lose by being a greedy gut now that his soul belongs to Satan."

"Not if he thinks he can get his soul back," Tom said. "Tomorrow he'll come to me and confess he broke his sacred vow and Satan sent a devil to claim his soul. I'll tell him the only way he can get his soul back and have God forgive him is to never eat any more candy, ice cream, or desserts again. He'll be so scared he will do it. I'll take twenty-six pounds off him in no time. That two dollars and sixty cents is as good as if it was in my pocket right now."

But Herbie didn't come to school Monday morning. When I told Tom about it at noon he seemed pleased.

"He is so darned scared he was too sick to go to school," Tom said.

But when Herbie didn't come to school on Tuesday either, Tom was worried. He and I went to the Sties home that afternoon.

"Is Herbie sick?" Tom asked Mrs. Sties when she opened the front door. "He hasn't been in school for two days."

"We don't know what's the matter with him," Mrs. Sties said. "He fainted Sunday night. He won't eat a thing. He won't leave his room. He seems frightened of something but he won't tell us what it is. If he isn't better by tomorrow morning we will have to call the doctor. I'll tell Herbie you called."

Tom was smiling as we walked home. "Did you hear that, J. D.?" he asked. "Herbie won't eat a thing. That should take off a few pounds."

My conscience began to bother me a little bit. "Maybe we should have told his mother the truth," I said. "She sure looked worried."

"The longer Herbie doesn't eat," Tom said, "the more weight he'll lose at ten cents a pound."

Herbie didn't come to school all that week. When Papa came home from the *Advocate* office on Friday he looked worried. Mamma met him in the parlor with the usual kiss. Then she stepped back and looked at him.

"What is bothering you, dear?" she asked.

"The Sties boy," Papa said. "I heard he was ill and thought I might put an item in the local news about it. I went to see Mr. Sties at the bank and then to talk to Dr.

LeRoy. The boy is suffering from some strange illness that Dr. LeRoy can't diagnose. He fainted last Sunday night and has refused to eat a bite since. If they try to force feed him the boy just spits the food out. And he is terribly frightened about something but he won't say what it is. It's so serious that Dr. LeRoy is going to have Mr. and Mrs. Sties take the boy to a hospital in Salt Lake City tomorrow."

Tom looked a little pale. "Is it that serious?" he asked.

"It is very serious," Papa said.

"Would it help if Dr. LeRoy knew what frightened Herbie?" Tom asked.

"That is the crux of the whole matter," Papa said. "It's as if the boy is afraid of being poisoned and won't eat." Then Papa clapped his hands to the sides of his head. "Oh, no," he cried. "Not you again."

"I was only trying to make Herbie lose some weight," Tom said. "I just wanted him to believe the Devil would claim his soul if he didn't stop eating candy, ice cream, and desserts. I didn't think it would make him so sick that he would have to be taken to a hospital in Salt Lake City."

Papa's cheeks puffed up until I thought his head would take off like a balloon. He staggered to his rocking chair and slumped down into it.

"What have I ever done to deserve a son like you?" he cried, still holding his head.

Then Mamma took over with her usual crisp manner in a crisis. "Tom Dennis," she said, "out with it, and I mean all of it."

Tom made a complete confession. Papa was so flabbergasted that he just sat there staring at Tom as if my brother had just confessed he'd murdered half the people in town. But not Mamma. She was just plain angry.

117

"Supper can wait," she said briskly and with plenty of authority. "Tom Dennis, you just march yourself up to the attic and get that red devil suit this minute. And John Dennis, you put on that costume. And don't dilly-dally doing it."

I knew Mamma was really angry when she called us by our first and middle names. "Why did you have to confess?" I asked Tom when we got to the attic. "We'll get the silent treatment for at least a month and probably lose our allowances for six months."

"What did you want me to do?" Tom asked. "Let Herbie die?"

That made me feel ashamed. "I'm sorry," I said. "I didn't mean it."

Dr. LeRoy was in the parlor when we returned. I was dressed in the red devil costume.

"We are going to call on Mr. and Mrs. Sties," Mamma said. "And you two are going to tell them everything and beg for their forgiveness."

Tom made a complete confession in the parlor of the Sties home. I thought Herbie's parents would be very angry. Instead they were so relieved to find out Herbie didn't have any strange disease that they forgave Tom and me.

Tom was looking plenty relieved himself. "I'd better go tell Herbie now," he said.

Mr. and Mrs. Sties looked at Dr. LeRoy who nodded. I walked with Tom to the door of Herbie's bedroom.

"You stay outside until I call you," Tom whispered. "I'll leave the door open so you can hear."

Tom entered the bedroom.

"Hello, Herbie," I heard him say.

118

"It's goodbye and not hello," Herbie said in a weak voice. "I'm going to die and my soul is going straight to Hell. I broke my sacred vow and Satan sent one of his devils to claim my soul."

"Is that why you haven't been eating?" Tom asked.

"I can't eat," Herbie said. "God is punishing me for breaking my sacred vow. He won't let me eat anything. The food sticks in my throat and I have to spit it out. God wants to starve me to death for breaking my sacred vow and being a greedy gut."

"You aren't going to die," Tom said. "I knew Danny Forester was buying you crackers and candy and meeting you behind the Community Church. I just wanted to throw a scare into you. That wasn't a real devil you saw Sunday night. That was J. D. dressed in a Halloween costume."

"Honest?" Herbie asked.

"Let me introduce you to the devil you saw," Tom said. Then he called, "You can come in now, J. D."

I entered the bedroom. Herbie looked terrible. His face was all sunk in and pale. He stared at me.

"Is . . . is that really you, John?" Herbie asked.

I took off the headpiece and mask. "It's me all right," I said. "Tom boosted me up. I'm the devil you saw Sunday night. You were bent over taking off your shoes. I knocked on the windowpane. You looked up and saw me. Then you stood up. I wiggled my finger at you and you fainted."

Tom looked at Herbie. "Satisfied it was J. D. and not a real devil you saw?" he asked.

"Then the sacred vow didn't count," Herbie said.

"How could it?" Tom asked. "Only a priest or a minister or a judge or a clerk of the court or somebody like that can

119

administer an oath on the Bible. It was just kid stuff. I just wanted you to believe it was a sacred vow to scare you into taking off some weight."

I guess Herbie was either so angry at Tom or so relieved to know his soul didn't belong to Satan that he sat up in bed and made up a poem right on the spot.

"You played a dirty trick on me
You and your Great Brain.
But you can bet your boots
You will never do it again.
I don't care how fat I get
And of that you can be sure.
I'll eat, and eat, and eat,
And then I'll eat some more."

Then Herbie cupped his hands to his lips and shouted, "Mother, I'm hungry and want something to eat."

When we got home Aunt Bertha had supper ready. After we ate and the supper dishes were washed and put away, we were all sitting in the parlor. I knew Tom was due for some punishment. But Papa always postponed the bad news until after supper so it wouldn't spoil anybody's appetite. I guess Tom was thinking of how to soften the punishment when he spoke.

"I just don't understand," he said to Papa, "why Herbie would rather be fat than take off some weight so he could play and have fun with other kids."

Papa knocked some ashes off his after-dinner cigar into an ashtray. He had a stern expression on his face.

"That is Herbie's business," he said, "and no concern of yours. Leave Herbie Sties the way he is."

"I should have made them weigh Herbie tonight," Tom said. "I'll bet he lost twenty pounds this week, and by rights Mr. Sties owes me ten cents for each pound Herbie lost."

"By rights," Papa said, "the only thing Mr. Sties owes you is a good tongue-lashing, and I'm sorry he didn't give it to you. But I promised him that I would punish you and J. D. for what you did. You are both getting a little too old for the silent treatment so I'll just take away your allowances for a month."

"But," I protested, "I didn't stand to make any profit on the deal. I was just doing T. D. a favor."

"When you put on that devil costume," Papa said, "and went to the Sties home and scared the daylights out of Herbie you made yourself an accomplice."

Frankie who had been listening looked at me. "What's an accomplice?" he asked.

"A darn fool," I answered.

CHAPTER EIGHT

Thirteen

I NEVER REALLY KNEW why the number 13 was an unlucky number until Tom's thirteenth birthday. His birthday came just a couple of weeks after Papa had handed down his punishment for what we had done to Herbie Sties. Tom invited all his friends to the party, and because girls invited him to their birthday parties, he had to invite them too.

Frankie and I couldn't attend because it was only for boys and girls near Tom's age. But we ate our fill of cake and ice cream in the kitchen. After everybody at the party had cake and ice cream they began playing games. But did they play good games like Pin-the-Tail-on-the-Donkey? Heck no.

Mamma came into the kitchen and she was smiling. "They are playing Post Office," she said to Aunt Bertha.

"And the boys agreed to it?" Aunt Bertha asked with surprise.

"The girls suggested it and the boys couldn't back out," Mamma said.

I'd heard about this terrible game. A girl went into a room by herself. Then she called out that she had a letter for a certain boy. But did she have a letter? Heck no. The letter meant she had a kiss for the boy and the poor fellow had to go into the room and kiss her. There was no way to back out without being a spoil-sport.

Mamma began laughing softly. "I've never seen so many blushing faces in my life," she said.

"It's a dirty trick for my money," I said. "A fellow gets invited to a birthday party and has to pay for it by kissing a girl."

"Tom D. is at an age now when he will start thinking about girls," Mamma said. "And playing Post Office is a lot of fun."

"Fun for the girls maybe," I said, "but awful for the fellows."

"I didn't see any of them refusing to go into the post office and call for his letter," Mamma said.

"They only did it because they are friends of Tom's," I said. "And I'm saying right now if we have to play Post Office at my birthday party when I'm thirteen I'm not going to my own party."

"You'll change your mind by then," Mamma said. Then she turned to Aunt Bertha. "That cute little Polly Reagan is certainly making eyes at Tom D."

Now I was beginning to understand why thirteen is an

123

unlucky number. A fellow who has never had anything to do with girls has to start kissing them just because somebody is thirteen years old.

But that was only the beginning. The next day after supper Tom, Frankie, and I did our homework. Then we went into the parlor where Papa, Mamma, and Aunt Bertha were sitting.

Papa pointed his after-dinner cigar at Tom. "Before you start playing some game or reading, you and I have to have a serious talk. You are now thirteen. When a boy becomes a teen-ager it is time for him to leave boyish pranks and games behind and assume the responsibilities of a young adult. As you know, I've been working nights at the *Advocate* because I have so much new business. You will report to me for work after school on school days and you'll work full time on Saturdays and during summer vacation."

Tom looked as if he'd just been sentenced to Devil's Island. "You mean I won't have any time to play?" he asked.

"You'll have as much time as I had when I was your age," Papa said. "I went to work for my father on the *Boylestown Gazette* the day after I became thirteen. He said it was time I started to earn my keep."

"But what about Sweyn?" Tom asked. "He has been working with you during summer vacations."

"Your brother wants to become a doctor," Papa said. "I've arranged with Dr. LeRoy for Sweyn to work as an orderly at the hospital this summer."

"What about the chores?" Tom asked.

"Frankie is old enough now to help J. D. do all of the chores," Papa answered.

"But I won't even be able to go swimming this summer," Tom protested.

"We'll have our slow days when you can take the afternoon off and go swimming," Papa said.

Tom stood up. "I don't have any choice, do I?" he said.

"Yes, you do," Papa said. "Mr. Thompson at the meat market is looking for a strong young boy to work as a delivery boy for him after school and during summer vacation. You can go to work for Mr. Thompson and I'll hire someone else to help me. But every boy your age should start working and you are no exception."

"I sure as heck don't want to be a delivery boy for Mr. Thompson," Tom said.

"Then it's settled," Papa said. "You will report for work tomorrow after school."

Boy, oh boy, thirteen is sure an unlucky number, especially for a kid. A fellow goes along playing and having fun and enjoying life for twelve years, and then all of a sudden he becomes a slave just because he has a birthday. I couldn't help feeling sorry for Tom. Maybe I should have felt sorry for myself for having to do all the chores with Frankie. But I didn't. Tom had bamboozled me into doing his share of the chores so many times that not having his help didn't bother me at all.

Papa breathed what sounded like a sigh of relief. "I'll keep you so busy you won't have time for any shennanigans," he said. "I've put up with your schemes until now because of your age. But today you are a young adult, and from now on you will conduct yourself accordingly."

I couldn't help thinking that now the truth was out. Papa wanted Tom where he could keep an eye on him so he couldn't pull off any more of his swindles. That should have made me happy because I'd been the victim of more of Tom's swindles than anyone else. But after a week passed things

125

seemed awfully dull with Tom working.

To make matters worse, there was Polly Reagan. She had been making eyes at Tom for about a year but he had always just ignored her. Now that he was thirteen, that changed too. I think she hypnotized him with that kiss when they played Post Office at the party. I knew he was a goner when I saw him carrying her books home from school. Any spare time Tom had he spent with Polly.

Papa kept Tom's nose to the grindstone, but he couldn't stop my brother from using his great brain. A week after Tom started working at the *Advocate* we were all in the parlor after supper. Tom stood with one elbow resting on the mantelpiece of the fireplace.

"Know something, Papa?" he said. "The type case is set up wrong."

Papa removed his cigar from his mouth. "You've only been a newspaperman for a week and already you are telling me that I don't know my business. The type case is set up alphabetically like all type cases."

"The fellow who started it sure was dumb," Tom said. "There is a vowel in every word. You use vowels more than any other letters. You have to hunt alphabetically to find them in the type box. What you should do is to put the type for the letters *a, e, i, o,* and *u* in five compartments at the top of the type case. That would make it twice as easy and twice as fast to find a vowel when you're setting type."

Papa looked surprised and then pleased. "I believe you have a good idea," he said.

"Don't you think the idea should be worth something?" Tom asked.

"You're right," Papa said. "And now that you've got a

girl and are working for me I think it's only fair to increase your allowance to fifty cents a week."

A lot of good that fifty cents did Tom. His money-loving heart must have gone to sleep under the spell Polly Reagan had placed on him. He squandered the money buying ice cream sodas at the drugstore for Polly.

A month passed without Tom pulling off one swindle. Life became very dull for me and for all the fellows. They complained there was no more excitement now that Tom was working. And I was lonesome too. I never realized how much I would miss Tom. I tried hanging around the *Advocate* office just to be near him. But Papa said I was in the way and distracting him and Tom from their work.

I began to dread the day I would become thirteen. Papa would put me to work and some girl would cast a spell on me. No wonder thirteen is an unlucky number.

Then one Sunday afternoon as I sat on the back porch steps with Tom he put his arm around my shoulders.

"I've got a business proposition for you, J. D.," he said.

Every time Tom had put his arm around my shoulders and started talking about a business proposition it had cost me money. But things had been so darn dull since Tom started working and seeing Polly that if he wanted to bet I couldn't jump over our barn, I would have taken the bet.

"It's a deal," I said.

"But I haven't even told you what the proposition is," Tom said.

"I don't care what it is," I said. "I'll take it."

I know it sounds crazy but I really didn't care, even if it cost me my shirt. I was so happy knowing Tom was back in business that nothing else mattered. Maybe being thirteen meant a boy had to take on the responsibilities of a young

128

adult. Maybe being thirteen meant a fellow had to go to work. Maybe being thirteen meant a fellow was sure to fall under the spell of some girl. But there wasn't anything, not even being thirteen, that could prevent Tom from using his great brain and his money-loving heart. I knew I'd be the victim, but it didn't matter. At least life would be exciting again.

About the Author and Artist

JOHN D. FITZGERALD was born in Utah and lived there until he left at eighteen to begin a series of interesting careers ranging from jazz drummer to foreign correspondent. His stories about The Great Brain are based on his own childhood experiences with a conniving elder brother named Tom.

Mr. Fitzgerald is also the author of several adult books, including *Papa Married a Mormon*. He and his wife now live in Titusville, Florida.

MERCER MAYER'S delightfully droll illustrations appear in all of *The Great Brain* books. He is also the author-illustrator of the five wordless *A Boy, A Dog and A Frog* books, *A Special Trick, There's a Nightmare in My Closet,* and many others.

Born in Little Rock, Arkansas, Mr. Mayer now lives with his wife in Roxbury, Connecticut.